SEARCHING FOR SUNSHINE

CRESTBROOK COVE

HOLLIE LUCKIE

Book Cover by Bookin' It Designs

Content Edited by Brittni Van | Overbooked Author Services LLC

Edited by Erica Rogers | Logophile Editing Service

Proofread by Caroline Palmier | Love and Edits

AUTHOR'S NOTE

Thank you so much for reading *Searching for Sunshine*. Stella and Wyatt's story is full of a little bit of chaos, spice, and all the found family you could want. However, there are a couple of heavier, more serious topics that are discussed throughout the book.

Searching for Sunshine contains mature content that may not be suitable for all audiences. For a full list of content warnings, flip to the content list at the back of the book. Please note this list may contain spoilers.

PLAYLIST

When the Sun Goes Down by Kenny Chesney
She Looks So Perfect by 5 Seconds of Summer
Barefoot Blue Jean Night by Jake Owen
Cruel Summer by Taylor Swift
Somewhere With You by Kenny Chesney
Sunny and 75 by Joe Nichols
Tell Me How You Like It by Florida Georgia Line
Runnin' On Sunshine by Jon Langston
Here's to Never Growing Up by Avril Lavigne
Ain't Nothing 'Bout You by Brooks and Dunn
Watermelon Sugar by Harry Styles
You Had To Be There by Megan Maroney and Kenny Chesney
Cruise by Florida Georgia Line
Nonsense by Sabrina Carpenter
If You Go Down (I'm Goin' Down Too) by Kelsea Ballerina
Anywhere With You by Jake Owen
Blank Space by Taylor Swift
Yippiee-Ki-Yay by Kesha and T-Pain

To anyone who's fighting to find your sunshine.
Never stop searching.

CHAPTER 1
STELLA

"Miss Hale, Principal Wilson needs to see you at the start of your planning period," the staticky voice of the school secretary blasts loudly through the archaic intercom system in my classroom.

"Yes, ma'am. Thanks, Mrs. Turner. I'll be there as soon as the bell rings," I yell before turning back to my class full of ninth grade students.

"Oh, Miss Hale, I didn't know teachers got called to the office too. What'd you do?" one of the girls in my class teases, and I smile at her.

"Yeah, Miss Hale's totally the trouble maker around here," a student across the hall argues sarcastically. "Y'all know she loves rules. Remember when she spent the entire second day of school going over the handbook. There's no way she did anything wrong."

I have to laugh at that because he's right. The district pushed out a ton of new rules at the beginning of the school year, and I thought it was important for them to be informed.

But this class of students has never let me forget it, and it's turned into something they love to tease me about.

"Whoa, whoa, guys it's all okay. I'm sure there's just some paperwork he needs me to look over, but enough about me. Next week is the last week of school so I need you to make sure you study the figurative language notes for your final exam and get those last projects turned in too. Let me know if you have any questions. See you all next week," I tell my class as the bell rings, and they pile out of my room.

After tucking my phone into my pocket and taking a sip of my favorite energy drink, I blow out a breath and head to the office. I feel my anxiety rise at being called in, but I remind myself it's probably over a referral I turned in last week.

"You can go on in. He's waiting for you," Mrs. Turner says, sending a small smile my way before answering the phone on her desk. I smile back at her before knocking on Principal Wilson's door.

"Miss Hale, come on in and have a seat," Principal Wilson says, gesturing to the small armchair across from his desk. He pauses for a moment, but before I can say anything, he continues. "I keep hearing great things about that classroom of yours. All the kids are talking about that field trip to see *Romeo and Juliet* that you took them on last month too."

"Thank you, Mr. Wilson. We had a really good time and I'm so excited they all got to participate," I say, waiting for him to get to the point and tell me why he really called me in.

"Of course. Well, I guess I should go ahead and get this conversation over with. As much as I don't want to do this, the district's given me no choice."

"Uh, okay? What's going on?" I ask, swallowing the nerves building in my chest.

Mr. Wilson gives me a sad smile before replying. "Well

Miss Hale, I'm sorry, but I wanted to let you know that the district will not be renewing your contract at the end of the school year. I know we still have about a week left in the school year, but I wanted to give you time to start looking for other arrangements. This also gives you time to resign if you'd like instead to keep it off your record."

I blink a few times, confident I didn't hear him right. "What? I'm sorry, have I missed something?"

"No, not at all, Miss Hale. I probably shouldn't tell you this, but to be honest, I'm an old man with a year left until retirement. I've spent the last ten years here, and I'm tired of seeing this district act in the best interest of the people in the office rather than kids in our classroom. The district is losing a number of teaching positions, and we're having to make a lot of cuts. I pushed for us to reallocate some funds to keep some of you, but there just isn't enough money to go around."

I stare at him in shock for another minute before I stutter, "But all of my observations and feedback for the last three years have been close to perfect. I've spent the last two summers rewriting the curriculum guides and organizing training for the other staff for free because they couldn't find someone else to do it. I've taken on all the clubs and extracurriculars you've asked me to." I pause and take a deep breath, as tears threaten to fill my eyes at the realization that I'll have to say goodbye to all the students and staff I've spent the last three years of my life with.

"You're right, Miss Hale. They have been. And I don't have words for how frustrated I am with this whole situation. The truth is our class sizes are going to skyrocket, and I know the solution of filling the gaps with online classes is not going to benefit any of our students. And I'll be the first to tell you that no part of me thinks that you and the other staff members we're losing are as replaceable as the district would like to believe. But since we have to make cuts and given the fact that this was your tenure year, my hands are tied. I'm so sorry. But once you have time to process this, I'll be happy to make some calls and help you find something else."

Wiping away the lone stray tear that managed to break free, I smile at him and straighten my shoulders. "I understand, Mr. Wilson. I really appreciate you letting me know. I'll have my resignation letter to you tomorrow, and I'll let you know if I need a reference. Thank you again."

"You're welcome, Miss Hale. Enjoy your weekend," he says, turning back to a stack of paperwork on his desk.

Defeated, I walk out of the office and smile weakly at Mrs. Turner as I head back to my classroom. At least it's the end of the day because I don't have the energy to teach another class after what just happened. I collapse into my desk and take a moment to look around the classroom that doesn't feel like mine anymore. Sure, the last three years have had their ups and downs, but I've worked so hard building relationships with my students and trying to create some fun memories for them in my class.

I'm not too worried about finding another teaching position, but since the whole district is downsizing, I realize I'll have to consider moving or committing to a pretty hefty commute for whatever new job I find. And that's without the challenge of finding administrators who are supportive.

It looks like this summer might be more stressful than I planned.

"Hey, sweet boy," I call out as I open the door to my apartment later that afternoon. My chocolate lab, Duke, runs out of my bedroom and jumps on my legs in excitement. Despite how shitty today has been, I can't help but smile as his tail beats against the side of the counter when I bend down to pet his stomach.

"There's my angel," I tell him, and his long tongue slides out to lick my arm causing me to giggle. I got Duke two years ago from the shelter while I was on summer break, and his silly behavior never fails to bring a smile to my face. "Were you a good boy today?"

He gives me a goofy grin, and I pat his stomach again before standing to grab his leash. "Come on, buddy. Let's go for a walk."

Duke barks in agreement, and I grab his leash to take him on a lap or two around the apartment complex. As I walk, I try to decompress after everything that's happened today. Before I can get too lost in thought, Duke pulls at his leash, reaching to grab a stick on the side of the sidewalk. He brings it to me, wagging his tail at his new find. My dog looks at me for a moment before dropping his new stick and sitting at my feet for me to pet him.

"You always know when I need some love, don't ya sweet boy?" I coo, bending down to his level and petting him again before leading him into the gated dog park in the apartment and throwing the stick for him to chase. We play for a while until he's panting and looking like he's ready for a nap. Re-clipping his leash, I pat his head before telling him, "Come on, buddy. Let's go home."

I'm walking back inside when I hear my phone ping with a text. Pulling it out, I see that it's Avery, my roommate and best friend from work.

Avery: Did you get the boot too?

Stella: Yep. They got you too, huh?

Avery: Sure did. Apparently the district doesn't think funding art and some of the other electives is necessary. Biggest load of bullshit I've ever heard.

Stella: *eye roll* I hate that. I guess we're job hunting together then?

Avery: Hell yeah we are. There's no way I can deal with all the craziness at school without you.

Stella: Sounds good. I'll start searching and see what I can find.

Avery: Perfect. I'm finalizing the set up for the art show next week and then I'll be home.

Stella: Okay. Dinner?

Avery: As long as there's also drinks, I'm in ;)

Stella: Deal.

I can't believe this is happening, I think to myself, throwing my phone on the bed and changing into my running clothes. I've spent the last three years devoting all of my energy to Smith's Valley High, and now what? I start over again in a new school? The thought makes my stomach hurt, so I try to focus my attention on getting ready for my run instead of the frustration and anxiety running through me at the thought of what the next few months may bring.

Running has always been my favorite way to unwind after a long day of work, and I definitely need something to take my frustration out on today.

After lacing up my running shoes, I grab my headphones and hit the trail behind the apartment. It takes me a little longer than normal to find my rhythm, but after a few songs, I settle into my easy pace. As I run, I go on autopilot and all the noise in my brain goes quiet for the next few miles. I didn't grow up in Smith's Valley, Alabama, but I've spent the last ten years here, and I have to admit that the thought of moving to a nearby city for work does make me a little sad.

Between losing my Memaw earlier this year—who was the closest thing I had to a parental figure after my parent's divorce—and now the loss of my job, I feel a little lost. My parents announced that they were separating the day after my high school graduation, and both of them rushed into new relationships, meaning I'd been all but forgotten by the time I moved into my dorm two months later. My Memaw was one of the only family members that I still had contact with, and that knowledge made her loss even harder.

I'd give anything to call her and get her advice on what to do right now, but I can hear her voice now. *"Oh, my sweet child, don't you know everything is going to work out? Life's a trip and it's time for you to enjoy the ride. And if you need some help, find yourself a hot guy and ride him too."*

Despite feeling my chest tighten with grief, I can't help but smile at the thought. Memaw was notorious for sprouting out some of the most inappropriate, silly things with a smile on her face. Shifting my attention back to my run, I focus on my pace for the last three miles. By the time I make it back to the apartment, I'm desperate for a shower, but I feel way better than I did seven miles ago.

"Damn, girl, hasn't your day been bad enough? Did you really need to torture yourself anymore running in this heat?" Avery teases, holding up her wine glass. "Couldn't you just have a glass of wine like the rest of us?"

"I figured I'd do both," I say with a laugh, grabbing my water bottle and taking a long swig before turning back to her. "I'm going to grab a quick shower, and then we can go get dinner."

"Sounds like the perfect end to a shitty day," Avery says, shimmying her shoulders.

CHAPTER 2
WYATT

"Motherfucker, will anything ever go right on this damn boat?" I mutter under my breath as the motor sputters to a sudden stop, causing the boat to lose power and jostling me and the rest of my passengers.

"Uh, man, I'm no mechanic or anything, but, uh…I don't think it's supposed to do that," one of the men I'm supposed to be taking out on a fishing trip says.

"Yeah, that didn't sound too good," his friend agrees.

As soon as this group stepped on the boat, they started offering "suggestions" of things I should do differently, despite the fact that when I asked, none of them had been on a boat more than once. I'll never understand what it is about a boat that makes other men act like they've lived on the water their entire lives. The attitudes of most of these groups get on my damn nerves, and even though it's been less than ten minutes since we left the dock, I'm already looking forward to this trip being over. However, I would much rather it conclude with a few happy customers and some decent tips for once.

I blow out a breath and try to hide my frustration. "It's probably something with the spark plugs. It shouldn't take me long to get it fixed, so y'all can hang out and wait. Or if you'd rather go on out, I can try to get one of our other boats to come get you and finish your trip."

"We don't mind waiting. As long as we don't run out of beer, I'm pretty sure we can keep ourselves entertained," one of them says before turning and grabbing a handful of beers out of the cooler for him and the others to shotgun. The rest of them cheer like their team just won the Super Bowl, and I fight the urge to roll my eyes at their antics.

"Fucking fabulous," I mumble, grabbing the toolbox I keep stashed away and turning to the back of the boat to work on the motor.

It takes me less than ten minutes to get the spark plug replaced and after making sure everything is ready to go, I turn back to my passengers.

"All right. Sorry about that. We're good to go now," I tell them, straightening and pointing us out toward one of my usual fishing spots.

"No big deal. Really, man, don't sweat it. We're having a great time," one of them calls back.

"Yeah, man, no stress. Do you want a beer or something?" another one of them asks.

"Nah, I appreciate it, though," I say tightly, turning back to the miles of open water.

Despite it feeling like nothing's going right today, I feel my frustration ease a little at the sight. The water's always been my favorite place, and now that we're easing back into the heat of the summer, I feel more at home out here than anywhere else.

"All right, we'll try this spot first," I explain, before grabbing the poles and sitting them out for the guys.

"So, what are we catching? Sharks?" one of the men asks with a goofy grin.

"Dude, you're a fucking idiot," another one says. "We're definitely catching largemouth bass."

I pause, waiting for either of them to laugh before I realize they're serious. "Largemouth bass are actually freshwater fish. At this depth, you'll be fishing for mostly red snapper. Let me give you a quick tutorial, and then you should be good to go."

I go through my usual spiel teaching them how to cast and reel their lines in before making sure they have everything they need. "All right, gentlemen, y'all can start whenever you're ready. Just make sure you watch out for each other when you're casting and don't jerk your line too hard so we don't get any stray hooks. I'll be here if you have any questions."

The men rush to get started, and I turn to grab my water. The best part of a fishing trip is once I get them going, I can let them do their own thing and only have to intervene to help them get the fish in the boat. I'm just sitting down to stay out of the way when I hear one of the men from the tour start screaming.

Alarmed, I run over to see that one of them managed to get his hook lodged in his friend's hand and there's blood everywhere. *Motherfucker.*

"Damn it," I mutter, reaching out and examining his hand. It's not the worst I've ever seen, but thanks to the barb that was on the hook, I don't feel comfortable pulling it out myself.

"Okay, gentlemen. I think this fishing trip's over," I say,

shaking my head and turning to the wheel to head back to shore.

Have I mentioned I'm over this fucking day?

"How was the trip today?" my brother, Trent, asks later that afternoon as I walk into our little shack at the marina.

"Well, it ended with me washing a shit ton of blood out of the *Fin and Tonic,* so I'll let you be the judge of that," I grumble, reaching for the fridge to grab a beer now that I'm done for the day.

"Damn," Trent mumbles, shaking his head. "How in the hell did that happen?"

"Well, to start, the boat fouled a spark plug less than ten minutes in and I had to fix the damn thing in the water, which you know is a real pain in the ass. Then, as soon as I got that fixed, I took them to start fishing, and one of 'em got hooked straight in the hand on their first fucking cast. So clearly it was a really great fucking day."

"Shit, man. That sucks. I guess since you didn't call me to tug you back, you got the boat up and running?" my brother asks.

"Yeah, thankfully it was a quick fix, but that's the second time this week she's given me trouble. I don't know what we're going to do if she goes out," I admit, and I know Trent doesn't miss the concern in my voice. "We already had to let both our deckhands go last month because we didn't have enough tours, and if things don't pick up soon, we'll be eating into the slim profits we've had so far this year."

My brother and I have run Crestbrook Charter Company

together for the last six years, and we've gotten used to the ups and downs of being small business owners. When our granny died, I convinced Trent we should use the inheritance we received to start the business. The idea of spending all day on the water and showing others how to fish seemed like a dream. But now that the business isn't doing as well as we'd like, I feel a ton of pressure to make sure Trent never regrets going into business with me. And sometimes, like today, the pressure just seems too damn much.

"It'll be fine. We've always figured it out in the past," Trent says with a shrug before picking up a stack of invoices from the small desk in the corner. "I do have to say the bills are adding up over here, but we're going into the summer season, so hopefully that'll give us the push we need."

"I hope you're right. But between the new charter service in the next town over that opened last year and all the upkeep we've needed this year, I'm worried we won't make it to another summer season."

"Let's not go there yet. Why don't we go get a drink from The Sand Bar and we can try to brainstorm some ideas to get some other business?"

"That sounds fine. I'm starving. Do you know if Everett's there tonight?" I ask, referring to our other brother who owns the local dive bar in town.

"You know he never leaves that place," Trent chuckles. "I'd tell him he needs to get out more, but then we might actually have to pay for our shit when he's not there."

"Yeah, you're right," I agree. "Let's see if we can figure all this shit out."

CHAPTER 3
STELLA

"Hi, I'm calling to speak to Miss Stella Hale," the voice through my car's speakerphone says as I attempt to merge through the crowded Smith's Valley High parking lot on the way home from work. Today was my last day at school, and I'm pretty sure it's been the longest day of my life.

"Speaking," I grumble, ignoring the honks from the teacher behind me as we all fight to get out of the narrow parking lot.

"Great. I was beginning to think we wouldn't ever be able to get a hold of you. We've been trying to contact you for the last week."

"Oh, I'm so sorry. I noticed a few missed calls this week, but I've been so busy with school, it completely slipped my mind. And I figured if it was super important you'd leave a voicemail or something," I say, not sure why I feel the need to defend myself. "Anyway, who am I speaking with?"

"My apologies, Miss Hale. I didn't mean for us to get off

on the wrong foot. I'm Mr. Marshall, and I'm the executor of your grandmother's will here in Crestbrook Cove," the man says, and I pause from where I was reaching to grab my energy drink from the cupholder.

"Wait? Are you talking about my Memaw?" I ask, feeling the familiar swell of grief rise inside of me at the reminder of the fact that my grandmother's gone.

"Well, the legal name of the deceased is Betty Hale, but I presume she was one and the same. And as for the estate, I have strict instructions from your grandmother to discuss this in person. Would it be possible for you to drive down to meet with me early next week?" the voice on the other end of the line asks, pulling me from my thoughts.

"Um, what? Drive to Crestbrook? Next week? Listen, sir, I don't mean to sound ungrateful but I have a lot going on here, so if you're calling me down there to tell me she left me her collection of smutty monster romances or something, I'm really grateful, but can you just mail them to me or something?"

"I assure you, Miss Hale, while I can't discuss the specifics over the phone, it will be well worth your time to make the trip, and I'd be lying if I said it wasn't a bit time-sensitive," Mr. Marshall says, and I note a hint of frustration in his voice.

After thinking for a second and realizing I don't have much of a choice, I finally say, "Okay, Mr. Marshall. I'll be there on Monday afternoon."

"I'll see you then, Miss Hale. You know where the old law office is here in Crestbrook, I presume?"

"Yeah, I do. I'll be there around three. Thanks again," I tell him as I end the call, fighting the urge to bury my head in my hands. I'd planned to start the job search on Monday since the realization that I have no clue what my life's going to look like in just a few months is causing me major anxiety, but obviously, that'll have to wait a little longer.

I try to imagine what on earth could be so important in Crestbrook Cove that I have to drive down in person, but my Memaw always had a flair for the dramatic. I'm not expecting much, but since I'm obviously not going to get answers over the phone, I may as well make the trip now before summer really starts.

I'm almost back to the apartment, still lost in my thoughts when my phone pings.

> Avery: HAPPY SUMMER! Now that we're both officially unemployed, how should we celebrate?

> Stella: Not sure that's really something to celebrate, but I'll drink to surviving the school year. Want to do takeout and seltzers by the pool?

> Avery: I'm in. Be home in an hour or two.

> Stella: Perfect. I'm going for a run and then we can order.

> Avery: Sounds good. See you in a bit.

I spent the morning taking my classroom apart and loading the boxes in my car to go into storage until I can decide what's next for me. I'm exhausted, and despite wanting to keep up with my training schedule, I know there's no way I'm making it more than a few miles today. As soon as I step into the apartment, Duke runs at me and I sit on the floor to pet him.

"Hey, buddy. Did you have a good day?" I ask, and he

licks my face in confirmation. "Good, my sweet boy. Let me go change clothes and we'll go for a quick walk before my run."

My lab's tail wags wildly, and he rolls on his back for me to rub his tummy. Smiling, I love on him for a few moments before standing. After changing, we make a few short laps around the apartment complex before I take him back inside. Despite being a pretty active pup, he's never enjoyed running with me, so I lace up my shoes and leave him snoozing on the couch as I head out for my run. My pace is slower than usual, but I still feel my anxiety lessen slightly the longer I go. After I hit my third mile, I slow to a walk and head back to my apartment.

"Hey, how was your run?" Avery asks as soon as I walk in the door. She's curled up on the couch with Duke at her feet, and I can't help but smile at the sight.

"It was good. I didn't go too far today, but I needed to clear my head. It's been a weird day, huh?"

"Tell me about it. I guess I should have expected it, but I didn't think I'd feel so sentimental leaving Smith's Valley High this afternoon," Avery confesses, running her fingers through her long blonde hair before tossing it into a bun on the top of her head.

I nod in agreement before walking across the apartment to the kitchen. "Yeah, I'm not gonna lie, some of the goodbyes were a little brutal. But I guess it makes sense. We have spent the last three years there."

"Yeah, you're right. But enough of that. I'm manifesting a fun, new adventure for us this year."

I laugh at that as I lean across the island to grab a glass to fix myself some water. "I'm in. I mean, honestly, I wouldn't mind a little more excitement. I've realized over the last few weeks that I feel a little stuck. I honestly don't remember the last time I did something fun and spontaneous."

"Same. But all of that's going to change this summer, I can feel it," Avery says seriously.

"Well, considering the fact that we're both about to be job searching and potentially moving, you're probably right." I laugh, taking a long sip of my water.

"Right, but isn't that all the more reason to see this whole summer as an adventure? Just promise me we'll say yes to whatever comes our way."

"Fine, I promise to say yes to things as long as it's reasonable," I agree, rolling my eyes.

"Nope, that's not good enough for me. You have to say yes to everything. No takebacks," my best friend insists, and I resist the urge to laugh at the serious expression on her face.

Avery's always been my most fearless friend, and she's always looking for an excuse to bring me out of my comfort zone. It's not that my life's particularly boring, but I'm happy with a quiet night in—preferably with a nineties romcom and a glass of wine. Avery, on the other hand, lives for dancing at the bar and taking shots of tequila. But somehow, our personalities manage to balance each other out, and I know better than to argue when she's so set on something.

"Okay, okay," I tell her, holding up my hands in a sign of surrender. "I promise. I'll say yes to whatever comes our way this summer. But if we end up in jail or in debt because of it, I'm never letting you hear the end of it."

Avery laughs at me. "I can live with that. Now, are you still on for drinks and takeout tonight?"

"Yeah, let's do it. Let me get changed and I'll meet you by the pool in a few minutes. Order us whatever you're feeling," I tell her, leaving her to cuddle with my dog while I throw on a swimsuit and cover up.

After I'm changed, I catch sight of my reflection in the mirror and pause to throw my long brown hair into a high ponytail. I pat Duke's head as he settles into his favorite spot on the couch and I check to make sure my tote bag has everything I need before heading down to meet Avery.

The small pool at our apartment is full of a mix of college students, singles, and young families all celebrating the start of summer, but after a moment of searching, I spot my best friend in the corner sitting on a lounge chair and make my way over.

"Looks like everybody else had the same idea we did, huh?" I tease, throwing my bag down and collapsing into the lounger beside her.

"You're telling me. I thought I was gonna have to fist fight the girls from the apartment across from us. They tried to steal your chair, but don't worry, I fought them off." Avery rolls her eyes before reaching down and handing me a black cherry seltzer from the cooler between us.

"I'm glad you took care of that for us. Anyway, here's to a summer of new beginnings." I hold up my seltzer and she taps her drink against mine.

"I'll drink to that," Avery teases, as we both take a long sip of our drink. After a moment I settle back into my seat and close my eyes as she asks me, "So, have you called your Uncle Allen about job options yet?"

"No, I need to do that this weekend I guess," I tell her, resisting the urge to sigh. My uncle is the principal at Springside High School, which is a small town about an hour and a half away, and I've considered calling him to see if he knows of any teaching opportunities in his area. I'm sure he'll do everything he can to help us, but I'm not thrilled about the idea of moving to a town that small. I've gotten used to living in Smith's Valley, and even though it's not a huge city, the college in the center of town ensures there's always something fun to do. Plus, I'm certain the dating pool in a town that small is nonexistent, which isn't exactly what this single girl is looking for. But I know if it comes down to it, Uncle Allen can probably help us find somewhere to work, and Avery and I could make the best of it for at least a year.

"Maybe we'll find something next week. I've got to go back to my classroom at Smith's Valley High on Monday to finish packing my room, but after that, we can start working on applications," Avery suggests.

"Yeah, that sounds good. I forgot to tell you, I have to go to Crestbrook Cove on Monday anyway," I tell her, taking a sip of my drink.

"What the hell, Stels? There's no way you're having a beach day without me," Avery yells, pulling her sunglasses down her nose to look at me in disbelief.

"No, no. I promise it's not anything fun. I've got to go meet with a lawyer. He called me today and said he had something urgent to discuss about my grandmother's will."

"Oh my god! Stella!" Avery shrieks loud enough that the people around the pool all turn to look at her. She shrugs at them before turning back to me and asking, "What the hell? Why are you just telling me this? What do you think it's all about?"

"Honestly, I have no idea. I'm sure it's probably nothing."

"Oh my goodness, what if she left you millions? We could finally take that trip to Europe we've been talking about."

"Aves, I love you, but Memaw didn't even have thousands—at least not as far as I know. She and my Pops spent pretty much everything they had on the hotel there in Crestbrook," I explain before adding, "so don't start booking any plane tickets or anything like that."

Memaw and Pops met when they were both working at

the High Tide Hideaway, and according to both of them, it was love at first sight. She was a housekeeper and he was a concierge the summer they met, but they both fell in love with the hotel as they spent time together. They worked their way up, and when the previous owner retired, they offered to sell it to them. But after Pops died several years ago, Memaw struggled to keep the place running by herself. The last time I talked to her, she was debating selling to a land developer from out of town who wanted to level the hotel and build a mansion on the beach. It was everything she and my pops had worked their whole lives to avoid, but with the cost of everything going up, she felt like she had no choice.

"Well, it's gotta be something big if he's making you drive all the way to Florida just to hear what he has to say."

"Aves, you're acting like it's an all-day trip. You and I both know it's two hours max. And plus, he said he was just following my grandmother's wishes. In case you forgot, she was known for being just a tad bit dramatic." I laugh.

"Yeah, I'll say. I'll never forget the first year we taught together and she showed up at the school in full Elizabethan attire because you told her you were teaching *Romeo and Juliet*," Avery teases, and I smile at the memory. "But do you need me to try to move things around to go with you? I don't want you to be by yourself if it's something sentimental."

"No, I'm sure I'll be fine. I'll probably be back before dinner, and then we can start to think about what we want to do next year," I offer, sipping my drink and flinching when one of the college boys jumps into the water beside our lounger and splashes us with water before turning back to wink at us.

"If you wanted attention that damn bad, you could've just asked, loser," Avery calls, rolling her eyes while she wipes the water from her glasses and turns back to look at me. "Okay fine, but you'll have to keep me updated while you're gone. And I still say if you want me to move things around to go with you, I totally will."

"No, I promise it's okay, but I appreciate it. I'm sure it's nothing. I'll go down and take care of this, and then our summer of adventure can begin. So, what do we want to order for dinner?"

CHAPTER 4
STELLA

"Hi, I'm here to see Mr. Marshall," I tell the receptionist as I step into the Marshall & Smith Law office on Monday afternoon.

She smiles warmly at me before gesturing to a small seating area in the corner of the room. "Of course, he told me we were expecting you. Just have a seat and he'll be with you shortly."

"Perfect, thank you," I answer, taking a seat and pulling out my phone to text Avery.

Stella: Made it to Crestbrook Cove. Meeting with the lawyer now and then I'll be home later tonight.

Avery: Sounds good. Don't forget I need all the details as soon as you know what's going on.

Stella: I'm still sure it's nothing but I'll make sure to let you know. See you in a few hours.

I've just hit send when one of the small office doors opens and the man I'm assuming is Mr. Marshall emerges. He looks to be in his late seventies, and his suit hangs awkwardly from his frail body. He hobbles over to me and offers me a stern smile before reaching out his hand to shake mine.

"Hi, Miss Hale. I appreciate you taking the time to meet with me at the last minute. I hope it wasn't too much of an inconvenience."

"Oh, it wasn't bad. I live in Alabama, but it's pretty close to the state line and the tourists don't seem to have descended yet, so traffic wasn't too bad," I tell him as he leads me into his office.

The room is so covered with books, boxes, and stacks of paper that I have to follow directly behind him through a path to his desk. I have no idea how he finds anything in here, but as soon as we sit down, he shuffles through a box behind his desk and pulls out a huge folder. After slamming it on the desk, he collapses into the overstuffed leather desk chair and looks over his wide-rimmed glasses at me before motioning for me to sit in the small wooden desk chair across from him.

As soon as I'm seated, he sighs and starts, "Listen, Miss Hale. I've got to be honest. Mrs. Betty was one of my favorite clients, and she did a lot for the town of Crestbrook Cove over the years. But as you know, your grandmother was a bit particular on how she wanted things done, and I'm afraid her will was no different. I'd be lying if I said I wasn't a little confused about her requests, but I promised her I'd fulfill her wishes. So let's get to it," he tells me, pulling an envelope out of the folder.

"Okay," I say hesitantly, feeling my anxiety rise at his tone.

"With that being said, your grandmother named you the sole proprietor of the High Tide Hideaway Hotel here in Crestbrook Cove, but that comes with provisions. In order to take over the hotel, you must agree to take full responsibility of the property for at least a year. You would be expected to live in the house behind the property and take on a full management role. If you should choose to decline the offer, the hotel will be sold to the land developers and the money from the sale will be donated to one of the local charities—if we can even find one of them willing to accept the money. The Hideaway is a local landmark, and this town has banded together for decades to keep these money-hungry developers out. I can't tell you what to do, but I urge you to think long and hard about how you want to handle this."

He pauses and I stare at him with my mouth open in shock. "I'm sorry, but you mean move to Crestbrook Cove full-time and take over the hotel?"

"Yes. There's also a small fund available for renovations to the property, and there's a handful of staff members who have been working to keep the hotel going since Betty's passing who I'm sure will be willing to help you should you decide to take on the responsibility," he continues, clearly oblivious to my shock.

"Uh, wow. Okay, I don't know what to say," I admit, still trying to get over my shock.

"I'm afraid there's a bit more to it, though," Mr. Marshall says with a wince.

"More?" I ask, feeling the blood drain from my face.

"Yes. Uh, in order to take over the Hideaway, your grandmother made the stipulation that you have to be married."

I freeze. "Married? I have to be married?"

Mr. Marshall shifts uncomfortably in his seat. "I'm afraid

so, Miss Hale. Your grandmother was also very thorough and specified that he must also reside in the cottage behind the hotel."

"No, no, no. There's no way. Do you realize I haven't been on a date in two years? How the hell am I supposed to find someone to marry?"

The lawyer across the desk shrugs at me. "I understand your shock, Miss Hale, but it is what it is."

"Is this even legal?" I ask, blinking as I try to process everything he's telling me.

"I'll be the first to admit it's a bit unusual, but it's not against the law. And we both know your grandmother was known for being unconventional."

I just stare at him for a moment before he continues, "But as I told you on the phone, this matter is a bit time-sensitive. Your grandmother stipulated that you'd have three months from her passing in order to make a decision, but considering the trouble we had contacting you, that deadline is coming up at the end of the week."

Unable to help myself, I burst into laughter. "Wait, wait, wait. So you're telling me that not only do I have to move to Crestbrook Cove, take over the hotel, and find a husband, but I have to do it all in the next five days?"

"I'm afraid that's correct," Mr. Marshall says apologetically. "I will say though, it's not my place to offer advice to you, but legally, your grandmother couldn't stipulate that you have to be in love. She just said you had to be married and live on the property for a year. If you can find a way to make that happen, then at the end of the one year mark the High Tide Hideaway is yours to do what you want to with. You can find someone to manage it, move away, sell it to someone local—whatever you think is right."

"Uh, yeah, I guess you're right," I tell him, trying to think of anyone I could recruit to take on the challenge of the next year with me, but I come up empty.

"And there's one more thing," the lawyer continues, and I fight the tears threatening my eyes.

"What? What else could there possibly be?" I explode, my usual calm and cheerful demeanor completely gone with the stress of everything he's just told me.

"Your grandmother left you a letter. I don't know what's inside it, but I think you should read it before you make a decision," he suggests, holding out the cream envelope he's held in his hands while we talked.

I take it with a shaking hand, unsure I'm capable of reading it with how fragile my emotions feel right now. Deciding to get it over with, I blow out a long breath before tearing the seal of the envelope and pulling out the letter. My eyes well with tears at the sight of her familiar loopy cursive, and I let them fall as I start to read.

> *My sweet Stella,*
>
> *It may be selfish of me to make such a big ask of you while you're in the prime years of your life, but I couldn't think of anyone in the world who would take better care of the Hideaway than you. I hope you don't hate me for the decisions I've made, but the hotel was your home for all those summers we spent together, and I wanted you to have the option to make it your home again. I know it's a lot to ask, but I do hope you'll consider continuing the legacy your Pops and I built over the last fifty years.*

I also hope that by the time you read this, I watched you walk down the aisle, and you're married to the man of your dreams so the marriage stipulation isn't a concern. But if that isn't the case, just know I didn't add this requirement out of spite. When your Pops died, I realized how impossible it was to run the place by myself, and I couldn't let you take that on because of an old hag like me.

No matter what you decide, just know I'm always proud of you and I'm always in your corner. I may not be physically here anymore, but I hope you think of me any time you feel the sea breeze on your face or the sand between your toes. Anytime you need someone to listen, I'm always here.

I love you always, my sweet girl.

Memaw

By the time I finish the note I'm fighting full-on sobs, but I try to pull myself together as I look back up at Mr. Marshall. He awkwardly digs into his desk drawer before pulling out a travel-sized case of tissues and handing me one.

"I know this was a lot to process, and I'm sorry for that, Miss Hale. I really do think your grandmother had good intentions with all of this, and I really hope you'll think long and hard about what you want to do. You can call my office tomorrow or Wednesday with a decision," the old man says, and I force a smile.

"Yes sir. I really appreciate it. I'll call you in the next few days when I've had time to wrap my brain around all of this.

Thank you," I tell him, trying to keep it together until I make it to my car.

The secretary smiles at me as I leave, and I'm distantly aware of her speaking to me, but all I can think about is making it out the front door. As soon as I feel the humid, salty air on my face I gulp in a few deep breaths and run to my car where I finally break into a fit of body-wracking sobs.

CHAPTER 5
WYATT

"Are you meeting us for dinner tonight?" Trent asks after we finish our last tour of the day.

The rides today went pretty well, but I got soaked earlier when I was cleaning the boat and I'm more than ready for the day to be over.

"Yeah, I guess so. I've got to go to the store, so the bar is probably my only choice if I want something other than chips or eggs. But I need to run by the apartment first and change. I'll just walk over to The Sand Bar when I get done," I tell him as we check the lines and rinse down the boats one more time before heading inside.

"That's fine. I'll tell Everett you're coming, and we'll see you then. Do you need anything else before I head out?" my brother asks, grabbing his wallet and keys from the desk drawer inside.

"Nope, I'll just close out the computers and make sure everything's ready for tomorrow. See you in a bit," I tell him, leaning over the desk to grab the laptop we use to keep track of bookings.

He leaves me to it, and I spend a few minutes writing out the schedule and splitting the few charters we have booked between Trent and I. Business is much slower than it used to be, and I try to ignore the surge of anxiety I feel from looking at the empty calendar for the next few weeks despite the fact that the summers have always been our busiest season.

Deciding that stressing over it isn't going to change anything, I shut down the computer and make sure everything is turned off before walking out to my truck. After spending a few minutes digging for the towel I keep in the backseat, I throw it across the seat and head to my apartment.

It doesn't take me long to grab a quick shower and change into dry clothes, and soon I'm relocking my apartment door and heading toward The Sand Bar. The weather in May is my favorite—warm enough to enjoy the outdoors, but the heat isn't quite unbearable yet. My apartment is less than a half mile from my brother's bar and I walk for a few minutes in silence, trying to come up with some ideas to help generate some business at work. I'm lost in thought when I register a whining noise to my left on the quiet street. I pause, looking around to see if I can figure out what I keep hearing, but nothing looks out of the ordinary.

After a moment, I realize the noise is coming from a car in front of the small law firm in town. I walk over, not sure what I'm expecting to find, but it certainly isn't Stella Hale crying in the front seat.

Mrs. Betty and my grandmother, Meredith, were best friends for years, and each summer when Stella came to stay in town, we were thrown together constantly. My grandmother stepped in to raise me and my brothers when my mom developed breast cancer and died just before my ninth birthday. Since it was rare for my granny to have friends with children our age, I always looked forward to spending the day at the Hideaway with Stella.

We were great friends back then, but I haven't seen Stella in over ten years, and I blink back the shock of seeing her after all this time. After a moment, I register the way she's crying and immediately panic that she's hurt.

"Stella? Are you okay? What's going on?" I ask yanking her door open, alarmed by the amount of tears I see pouring down her face.

I don't know why I always had such a soft spot for Stella, but I have for as long as I can remember. The first time we met, she was near tears because a few of the hotel guest's children had been mean to her and wouldn't let her play with them. After that moment, I always felt fiercely protective of her when she visited over the summer. It's weird that I'm finding her in such a similar state, but I feel that same urge to help her rise up inside me at the sight of her tears.

She looks up, and a look of terror passes over her face before she realizes who I am. "Wy- Wy- Wyatt?" she stutters, rushing to wipe the tears from her eyes.

"Yeah, Stella, please tell me why you're so upset. And what are you doing in Crestbrook Cove? Did I miss that you're living here now?" I ask, vaguely aware I'm asking too many questions, but I'm so caught off guard I can't help myself.

"I—I—I came to meet with Mr. M—M—Marshall an-and he said that I—I need to t—take over the H-Hideaway and get mar—married," she says between sobs. Her body shakes with the tears and she's crying so hard she has to gasp for breath between each one.

"Stella, wait. I need you to calm down. Take a few deep breaths for me, okay?" I say, trying to keep my voice steady as she continues to cry.

"I just don—don't know where I-I went wrong," she cries and her breaths quicken again as she continues to get worked up.

I kneel on the ground so I'm at eye level with her and grab her hands. "Stella, look at me. We can figure out whatever it is that's going on, but for right now I just need you to breathe."

Her smaller hands shake in mine as she takes a few small breaths before muttering, "I feel—like I'm gonna—have a-a panic attack. Meds—in th-the back seat."

I jump up and open the back door looking for the meds she was talking about before grabbing the small prescription bottle and holding it out for her to take.

"I—I'm sorry," she pants, taking one of the small pills before leaning her head back against the headrest and closing her eyes. She continues to cry and take deep breaths as I kneel back on the ground and lean against her open door.

"You're going to be okay, Stella," I tell her, making sure to keep my voice gentle. "Just breathe and then you can try to tell me exactly what's going on."

We sit like that for a while in silence. I'm vaguely aware of my phone vibrating repeatedly in my pocket, and I pull it out to make sure everything's okay while I wait for her medicine to kick in. I roll my eyes when I see that I have more than twenty missed texts and calls from my brothers, and I scowl as I turn my phone off until I have time to talk to them. "Sorry, my damn family won't leave me alone," I murmur, tucking my phone back into my pocket.

Finally, she finally calms down enough to talk. "God, Wyatt. I'm so sorry. You must think I'm a complete disaster. You haven't seen me in years and then you walk by me having a complete meltdown in my car. And I'm sure you have somewhere to be."

She laughs weakly before reaching out to tousle my hair. "God, some things never change. Wyatt Robinson—always here to save the day. But no, really, thank you. It's been a long time since I felt the start of a panic attack that bad, and I really appreciate you talking me through it. But unless you have an idea to help me find a husband in the next five days, I don't think there's anything you can do."

I lift my eyebrows, trying to figure out what she means. "Husband? I'm sorry, Stella, but I'm completely lost. What's happened that made you so upset?"

"Well, I drove down today because Mr. Marshall called me last week and said he had something urgent to discuss with me in person about my grandmother's will. I thought it was going to be something minor like those books she loved to read or the creepy dolls she kept around to scare the extra bratty preteen guests back when we were growing up."

"Oh my god, how did I forget about those? Remember when she and my grandmother set one up in my room after my brothers and I told her we didn't want to come to her weekly lunches? I woke up and found it looking at me through the window in the middle of a thunderstorm, and every time the lightning flashed I was convinced there was someone looking in the window. It's been fifteen years and I still have nightmares about that thing."

Stella laughs at that before nodding. "Yeah, she did something similar to me when I refused to stop texting at the dinner table while I was in high school. It's definitely one of those memories that sticks with you."

"Right, but anyway, so you met with Bernard?" I ask, and she lifts her eyebrows at me in question.

"Who the hell is Bernard?" she asks and I fight the urge to laugh at her bewildered expression.

"Bernard Marshall—he's the lawyer you said you met

with. Sorry, in a town this small you've gotta remember that everyone is pretty much on a first name basis. He moved here a few years after you stopped visiting."

"Oh, gotcha. But yeah, I met with him and he started going over the stipulations of the will. And apparently, Memaw left me the High Tide Hideaway."

"Wait, Stella, that's awesome. So you are moving back? I know you always loved that place when we were growing up."

She winces at my words and sighs. "I wish it were that simple. My grandmother left some pretty specific requirements, and as much as I want to make it work, I don't know how."

"I'm sure you can figure it out. What exactly are the requirements?"

"Well, I've gotta move here immediately and live on the property for at least a year. Which, now that I've calmed down, isn't that big of a deal. I lost my teaching job last week, so it's kinda coming at a pretty good time," she rambles before continuing, "but she also added a stipulation that I have to be married in order to take over. And apparently, they had a hard time getting a hold of me so the deadline is the end of this week."

I wince, finally understanding why she's so upset. "Stella, that's wild. I'm sure you can find a way to fight it."

"Maybe you're right. But if I don't get married by the end of the week, the Hideaway will be sold to a developer and they'll tear it down. So I'm out of time. And plus, Memaw left me a note explaining her reasoning, and a part of me will always feel like I'm going against her last wishes if I don't do it her way, you know? But really, none of that matters, because I'm definitely not married. I'm going to have to let the place she and my pops worked their whole lives to build turn into rubble because I can't find a husband," she says, tears welling in her eyes.

I'm not usually an impulsive person, but as I watch her cry, my protective instincts rise and I don't take the time to think. Before my mind can catch up, I decide to just go with it.

"Why don't you just marry me?"

CHAPTER 6
STELLA

blink at him in shock, confident that I've heard him wrong.

"What? Us? Get married? I really appreciate you sitting with me while I calm down, but I'm still not really in the mood to joke about this." I sigh, bewildered by the suggestion.

Wyatt and I spent almost all of our free time together for years during my summer visits, riding our bikes around town and playing volleyball on the beach. But at the same time, I haven't seen him in almost ten years. I didn't realize how much I'd missed him until now, and I feel a rush run through me as I think about what he's offering. But this is silly—there's no way he seriously wants to get married to me in less than a week.

"I'm not joking," he says, his eyes serious. "Think about it—we already know each other. I already live in Crestbrook Cove, so my job and family are both here anyway. And honestly, my business thrives on the hotel doing well too. So this could be a win for the both of us."

"I don't think you understand," I insist, desperate not to get my hopes up. "My grandmother made it a stipulation that whoever I marry has to live on the property too. You'd have to move into the cottage behind the Hideaway with me. I can't ask you to do that."

He shrugs, looking far too calm for the seriousness of the conversation we're currently having. "That's fine. My lease in my apartment is up next month, and that lets me save some money that I can put toward my business. My brother and I run Crestbrook Charter Company, and honestly, we're struggling to keep things afloat at the moment."

I stare at him for a second, trying to gauge if he's really considering this. "You're serious, huh?"

"Sure, I don't see why not."

"Okay, let's just say for a moment that I'm considering this. Obviously, I know what I get out of this, but what's in it for you?"

"Well, for one, I actually really loved and respected your grandparents, and the last thing I want to see is the High Tide Hideaway in the hands of someone who only wants to tear it down."

I think about it for a minute before responding, "I guess that makes sense. But this is crazy, right? We can't just get married."

Wyatt smiles, and I take the time to really look at him for the first time now that I've calmed down a little bit. Between his long brown hair and his muscular frame, I'd be lying if I said he wasn't attractive. Can I really live with this man for the next year if it means keeping the hotel?

"I don't see why we can't," Wyatt says, pulling me from my thoughts. "I can call Mary at the county clerk's office and get the license taken care of, and I'm pretty sure one of my brothers can get ordained in a few minutes. We don't even have to go to the courthouse."

"Wyatt, I really don't think I can go through with this. I think I'm just going to have to tell Mr. Marshall that I can't make it happen this fast."

"Is that what you want?" Wyatt asks, and I feel the tears start to well in my eyes again at the question.

"No, but what option do I have? We can't just get married. We don't even know each other anymore."

He's quiet for a moment before he says, "You're right. But I do know this—I know that you loved your grandmother more than almost anything in this world. If you truly don't want to get married or you don't want the responsibility of taking over the hotel, there's nothing wrong with that. But if you're only saying no to this because you're scared, I'm afraid you'll always regret it."

I feel the tears start to fall again, and I hurry to wipe them. "God, I'm a disaster. But I know you're right. I just don't know what to do."

"I know, and I'm sorry you're having to make this decision so suddenly. But if you decide you want to do this, then we'll make it work. There's no pressure. We spend the year as friends who happen to be married, and at the end of the year, we can get a divorce and go on with our lives. It'll be like it never happened," he says calmly, and I realize he's right.

This isn't how I saw my life going, but when he puts it like that, I realize this does seem like the best option. It's not like we're gonna fall madly in love or anything. It's the equivalent of making any other business decision, except we have to live together. And the more I think about it, I'd probably feel safer living in the same cottage with him than some random guy I barely know. We may not have seen each other in a while, but I can tell just by the way he's treated me tonight that he's still the guy I was friends with growing up.

Realizing I don't really have any option outside of selling the Hideaway, I clarify, "Just as friends? No other expectations? And just for a year?"

Wyatt shakes his head. "Yep, just friends. And when all of this is over, we'll be the most amicable divorced couple this town has ever seen."

I laugh weakly at his joke, before responding, "Damn it, this wasn't really what I had in mind when I promised Avery to say yes to everything this summer," I mutter under my breath, and Wyatt gives me a look of confusion.

"I'll let you explain that one to me later," he teases before his face becomes more serious. "So, what do you say? Are we getting married this week, Stella Hale?"

I think about it for a long moment before I take a deep breath. "I guess I'm down if you are," I say before breaking into a fit of giggles. "Oh my god, this is wild. I can't believe we're really doing this."

Wyatt leans across my seat and grabs my phone from the cupholder. "My grandmother always said everything's an adventure with a Hale woman, so it seems pretty fitting. I'm putting my new number in your phone so you have it, and we'll work out the details tomorrow when you've had a little bit of time to process everything."

He looks down at my phone and looks at me in surprise. "Whoever this Avery person is really wants to talk to you. There are at least twenty notifications here."

I laugh, suddenly realizing I never called her back after I left the law office. "Oh gosh, she's my best friend. I was supposed to call her as soon as I got done with my meeting. She's going to kill me. Oh well, I'll call her back as soon as I get on the road."

"I figured you didn't come to this meeting prepared to move your whole life down here. Will you need help moving? I'm assuming you're still living in Alabama?" he asks as he adds his phone number to my phone before handing it back to me.

"No, it shouldn't be too bad. I don't think I'll have that much to pack. And yeah, I'm still in Smith's Valley. I'll drive back tonight and get all of that sorted out and plan to come back Wednesday night. I guess we can get married on Thursday since everything has to be finalized by Friday. You can take your time moving in if you need to, though."

"That works for me. Are you sure you're okay to drive back by yourself? I know today's been a lot."

"Yeah, I'm good. I still can't believe all of this is happening," I say with a laugh. "Are you really sure you're up for all this?"

"Yeah, Stella, I promise I'm good with it. Now, go ahead and get on the road, and I'll see you later this week," Wyatt tells me.

"Sounds good. Thank you, Wyatt."

He smiles at me and stands before closing my door and waving at me as I crank my car.

As soon as I pull out of the parking spot, I grab my phone. Preparing myself for Avery's reaction, I hit her contact and wait for her to answer through my car speaker.

"Stella Elizabeth Hale. What the actual hell is going on? I've been calling you for over an hour. I was getting ready to drive down there and check on you."

"Oh my god, Aves, I'm so sorry. It's been the wildest day ever," I tell her honestly.

"First of all, are you okay? I knew I should have come with you," Avery says.

"I'm okay now. But buckle up, because, girl, do I have a story for you."

"I swear to god if you don't spill, Stella, I'm gonna come unglued. What's the verdict? Are we gonna be sipping champagne in France this summer or what?"

I laugh and shake my head at her antics. "Not quite. Okay, I'll be honest: I don't know where to start but here it goes. Turns out, Memaw left me the High Tide Hideaway but in order to claim it, I have to move to Crestbrook Cove for at least a year and live on the property. Oh, and I have to be married too. But don't worry, I've gotten that part taken care of, and the wedding's on Thursday."

The line goes quiet for a moment, and I check my phone screen to see if I lost her. "Avery? You there?"

"What the actual fuck, Stels? You're joking, aren't you? I swear if you're joking I'm hiding your running shoes until you find a way to make it up to me."

"Aves, I swear I wish I was joking. I told you it's been quite a day."

"Okay, wait, you're serious. I'm gonna need you to rewind this all the way back and talk me through exactly what happened."

I spend the next twenty minutes telling her about the meeting with Mr. Marshall, Memaw's last wishes, my panic attack, and Wyatt's offer. I lose track of the number of times she interrupts me. Finally, when she's completely caught up, I finish with, "So, yeah, this isn't quite how I saw the summer going, but I guess it'll definitely be an adventure."

"Holy shit, Stella. I didn't think things like this happened in real life. I'm all for the main character energy you're channeling right now, but this is wild," Avery exclaims, and I can't help but laugh at the absurdity of it all.

"Yeah, I guess you're right. I just know Memaw had to be freaking giddy over this last round of shenanigans she orchestrated."

Avery laughs before agreeing. "Yeah, honestly if anyone could make all of this happen, it was her. So when do we move?"

I blink in surprise for a moment before responding, "We? Avery, I can't ask you to move to Crestbrook Cove with me. Where will you live? Where will you work? Just because I have to rearrange my whole life doesn't mean you have to."

"Babes, it's really cute you think there's anything that could stop me from moving with you. And as for where I'm going to live, didn't you just tell me you inherited a big-ass hotel? You can hire me to manage your marketing and event planning, in exchange for a place to stay. Plus, you know I've been wanting to get my art business off the ground, and this will give me time to do that for some extra money."

I feel my eyes well in my eyes at her offer and I feel my anxiety lessen a little at the realization that I don't have to do this all by myself. "Have I told you lately how much I love you? But really, are you sure you want to do this? From what Memaw told me last summer, we're gonna have our work cut out for us with this place."

"Back at ya, Stels. And yes, I'm sure. Looks like we were right about this being our summer of adventure, huh?"

"God, I've gotta say that I think this is a little more than I bargained for."

"Right? I still cannot believe you're getting married this week. Don't think you're off the hook from telling me more about this Wyatt guy, though," Avery teases before asking, "how far out are you? You promise you're still good to drive? I'm worried about you."

"No, I promise I'm good now. I should be home in about forty-five minutes," I tell her after double-checking my navigation app.

"Perfect, I'll order pizza and grab us a bottle of wine. Looks like we're going to have a few late nights this week. You and I have a wedding to plan."

CHAPTER 7
WYATT

"Man, where the hell have you been? I've been calling your phone constantly for the last hour," Trent yells as soon as I open the door to The Sand Bar.

"Shit, sorry. I got caught up on the way here," I explain, walking over to the bar where he's sitting.

"Caught up? There's less than a mile between here and your apartment. What in the hell happened?" Trent asks, making it clear he's not letting the topic go.

I'm just opening my mouth to respond when Everett, my other brother and the owner of The Sand Bar, comes out of the stockroom in the back with a new bottle of whiskey.

"Hey, Wyatt, where have you been? Trent told me you were coming over an hour ago."

"Well, I—" I start as Bennett, my best friend, walks over from where he was playing pool in the corner. Bennett and I have been friends as long as I can remember, and he runs the local surf shop here in town. He's like another brother to me, and we usually meet up at least once a week for dinner, but I didn't realize he was coming here tonight. Great.

"Hey, Wyatt, what took you so long? Trent told me you'd be here an hour ago," he says, interrupting me.

"Holy shit. I didn't know my whereabouts were such a big fucking deal," I mutter, rubbing my hand over my eyes in frustration.

"Come on, man, don't be a dick. You just weren't answering anyone's calls, and it's not like you to be late. Everything okay?" Bennett asks, leaning against the bar while Everett grabs us all a beer out of the cooler.

I wince, realizing he's right, before answering, "Yeah, everything's fine. But I guess I do have some news. I wouldn't make a big deal about it, but as soon as the news gets out this town is gonna go fucking nuts, and I'll probably need y'all's help anyway."

Trent raises his eyebrows at me waiting for me to continue. "Uh, dude, what the hell happened?"

Bracing myself for their reactions, I sigh. "I'm getting married on Thursday. And I'm moving into the High Tide Hideaway for the next year."

Both my brothers and best friend stare at me for a moment before they all burst into laughter.

"Damn, man, I know you're not usually one for jokes, but that's fucking hilarious. But in the future, you're gonna want to make your pranks a little more realistic. Getting married on Thursday. That's a good one, man," Trent says before they all look up at me.

They must see something on my face, because after a moment Trent tells me. "Okay, joke's over. You can laugh now."

"I'm not joking," I tell him, and the whole table freezes.

After a few seconds of awkward silence, Bennett's the first

one to speak. "Uh, what? I don't think I heard you right. Did you just say you're getting married?"

"Yeah, I've only had two beers, but I must be a little tipsier than I realized because that's what I thought you said too," Trent says, scratching his head in confusion.

"Uh, I'm pretty damn sober, and I heard the same thing," Everett interjects, and all three of them turn back to look at me.

"We're going to need a whole hell of a lot more explanation on this one, Wyatt," Bennett says, and Trent and Everett both murmur in agreement.

"Okay, fine. Do y'all remember Stella Hale?" I ask my brothers and they nod. I turn back to Bennett to explain, "Stella was Mrs. Betty's granddaughter."

"The one who ran the Hideaway for years, right?" Bennett asks.

"Yeah, that's her. I know you weren't always around during the summers while we were growing up, but our grandmothers were best friends. Stella came to stay with Betty every summer and since we were already living with our grandmother at that point, we spent a lot of time together."

"God, the two of you were basically attached at the hip when she was in town. I remember our grandmother always told us that you had the biggest crush on her," Everett says with a laugh, and I can't resist the urge to roll my eyes at my younger brother.

"I did not have a crush. We were just friends," I argue, turning back to my best friend.

"Basically, it started because our grandmother and Betty had a weekly lunch date. Even when they were taking care of us all, they only brought us along so they could see each other. And over the years, we just stayed friends when Stella was in town. Our grandmother volunteered us for odd jobs at the hotel as we got older, and Stella always kept us company because she didn't know a ton of people in town."

"Yeah, I think I remember meeting her one summer."

"That sounds right. Well, anyway, we all know Mrs. Betty died a few months ago, but Stella only found out today that her grandmother left her the Hideaway in her will."

"Okayyy," Everett says, dragging out the word. "That's great and all, but I don't understand what this has to do with you getting married. We haven't seen Stella in what? Ten years?"

"I'm getting there, okay? Betty left her the hotel, but there were some strings attached. In order for her to take over, she has to be married and she has to agree to live on the property and manage it with her husband for at least a year. Otherwise, she forfeits the place and it gets sold to some money-hungry land developer."

"Damn, that sucks, man," Trent says. "But have I missed something? I don't mean to sound like a dick but what does this have to do with you?"

"Yeah, I mean, have the two of you stayed in touch? How did you even find out about all of this?" Everett asks.

"No, I haven't seen her in years either. But when I was walking over here, I ran into her. I could tell she was upset, and once we started talking she told me everything. So I just suggested we get married."

My brothers and best friend all stare at me again, before Everett asks, "Wait, wait, wait. So not only are you getting married, but it was your idea?"

"Uh, yeah…" I answer, hoping they'll let this go but knowing that's pretty unlikely. The three of them are my best friends in the world and I can appreciate why they're worried about such a big announcement out of the blue, but I'm not in the mood to spend the rest of the night defending my decisions. And to be honest, I'm still not really sure why I offered to go through with all of this, but seeing Stella reminded me of everything my grandmother did for my brothers and me—andI know that this is something Betty and my grandmother, Meredith, would have wanted. Plus, if I'm being truthful with myself, I always liked Stella, and I couldn't stand to keep seeing her as upset as she was earlier tonight when I knew I could fix it.

"So you saw this girl for the first time in ten years and immediately offered to marry her and move in with her? The same guy who hasn't been on a date in over a year?" Trent asks incredulously.

"Yeah, I mean I know you're trying to help her out, and I think that's great. But you're also pretty much the least spontaneous person I've ever met," Bennett says, and I have to admit he's right. "Are you sure this is something you want to do?"

"Yeah, I'm sure. Listen, I'm not trying to make light of the situation, but it doesn't have to be a big deal. We spend the year married as friends, and then as soon as the year's over we get a divorce and she keeps the Hideaway," I tell them, taking a sip of my beer.

"Okay, that's your decision. And I always liked Stella. I think we're just surprised," Everett says, and the others nod in agreement.

"Yeah, it's safe to say that none of this was really on my bingo card for the year either," I mutter under my breath and all three of them chuckle before I continue. "But I promise I'm good. I think this'll be good for all of us."

"Okay, well, if you're happy, we're happy," Bennett tells me.

"Good, because I'm going to need a favor or two from y'all to make this work."

All three of them look at me, waiting for me to elaborate. "Yeah, man, whatever you need, we'll make it happen," Trent says, and I don't miss the uncertainty in his voice.

"Cool. In that case, I'll let y'all flip a coin to decide which one of you is getting ordained online to marry us. Oh, and we'll probably need help getting moved into the Hideaway later this week too."

"Damn, I hate moving shit," Bennett says then adds, "but sure. Between all of us, I'm sure it won't take us too long to get it knocked out."

"God, you were right earlier. The people of Crestbrook are going to lose their shit when they hear about this," Everett says, and I groan at the reminder.

"Shit, I'm not looking forward to that. I just wish everyone in this damn town would mind their own business," I mutter. I'm already imagining Miss Agatha, the town's busybody, tracking me down for all the details as soon as the news starts to spread. I love Crestbrook, but despite living here my whole life, I still don't think I'll ever be used to how fast gossip spreads around this place.

"Yeah, right. We all know better than that. You'll be lucky if you make it through this dinner before Miss Agatha has a marriage announcement on *The Cove Column*'s social media page," Trent teases. *The Cove Column* is the local newspaper that Miss Agatha runs, but she likes to drop some other town gossip on slow news days on the social media pages.

"You know, for being in her seventies, she's incredibly tech-savvy," Bennett muses.

"Okay, enough about weddings and Miss Agatha. Can we talk about something else now?" I ask, shifting my attention to Everett. "Also, can I get a burger or something? I'm fucking starving."

"I put your usual in the computer when I grabbed your beer. It should be ready in a few minutes. Trent and Bennett already ate since you took forever to show up."

"Thanks," I mumble, tipping up my bottle for another sip of my beer.

"So, Wyatt, Trent said that you've been having problems out on the *Fin and Tonic*. Do you think she's good to go now?" Bennett asks.

"Yeah, I hope she's good to go for a little while because I sure as shit don't have the extra cash to fix anything major," I admit as I pull my phone out of my pocket.

"Sure, now you decide to check the damn phone," Trent mumbles. I flip him off in response before turning my attention back to my cell. I have a text from an unknown number, and it takes me a moment to realize it's from Stella.

> Stella: Hey, it's Stella. I realized when I got home I never gave you my cell number. Just wanted you to have it in case you come to your senses and realize this plan is probably a terrible idea. Either way, thank you for taking care of me today.

> Wyatt: Hey, Stella. I have no intention of changing my mind, but I'm glad you texted. And no worries. Did you make it home okay?

> Stella: Yeah, I'm home now. About to start packing our apartment. Another plot twist— my best friend is going to move down to Crestbrook too. She'll be living in the hotel for a little while.

Wyatt: Oh, that works out. I've already got a moving crew ready to help y'all when you get here.

Stella: Look at you swooping in and saving the day again. I guess that's the theme of the day, huh?

Wyatt: No problem.

Stella: Okay, I've gotta get started on packing but I'll see you Wednesday evening before the wedding.

Wyatt: That sounds good. I'll see you then, Stella.

"Oh my god, Wyatt, are you seriously smiling at your phone screen right now?" Trent asks, staring at me from across the table.

"He definitely doesn't look that happy when he's texting us," Bennett jokes.

"Fuck off," I mutter, flipping them off as I tuck my phone in my pocket.

"Yeah, I feel like this summer just got a whole hell of a lot more interesting," Trent says, and I try to ignore the feeling that he might be right.

CHAPTER 8
STELLA

"All right, I think that's everything," I say, looking around the apartment Avery and I have shared for the last three years.

"I think so too. Thank god this place came partially furnished or we never would have managed to get all of our shit in our cars."

"Yeah, you're right about that," I agree before looking down where Duke is lying at my feet. "You ready for a new adventure, buddy? You're gonna be the cutest little beach pup Crestbrook's ever seen, aren't ya?"

His tail thumps against the floor as he rolls over for me to lean down and pat his stomach. "I know, it's gonna be so good, sweet Duke."

He licks my hand in agreement, and I stand, turning back to Avery. "I guess we're really doing this, huh?"

"Hell yeah, we are," Avery says, reaching over to grab Duke's leash from the counter and handing it out to me. "Are you ready to get out of here?"

"Yeah, I guess it's time. God, this is getting so real. I feel like I'm going to throw up," I mutter, taking a deep breath.

"Hey, hey, hey, Stels. Calm down," Avery says, reaching out to give me a hug. "It's all gonna be great. We're going to get in the car and we're going to start this new life in Crestbrook."

"I know, you're right. I just cannot believe I'm getting married tomorrow, Aves. I mean I know people get married all the time, but I always imagined my wedding day would be something special—not something thrown together in less than a week. And certainly not to someone who remembers all of my awkward phases or who I haven't seen since we were teenagers. Don't get me wrong, I know none of this is real, but it just feels like so much to take in."

"I think that's completely valid, babes. But just remember, you're doing what you have to in order to keep the hotel. And you're getting married to someone who you apparently used to be great friends with. Which, by the way, if you weren't already dealing with a lot of shit this week, I'd be totally pissed that you never told me you had some hot beach bestie growing up."

I roll my eyes at her and laugh, momentarily distracted from my anxiety over the move. "Aves, you're being ridiculous. Are you forgetting the part where I haven't seen him in literally forever?"

"Fine, fine. I'll give you a pass this time, but if I find out there are any other sexy singles in your past you haven't told me about, I'm never going to let you hear the end of it."

"Avery, you haven't even seen him yet. How do you know he's hot?" I tease, clipping Duke's leash onto his collar.

"Babes, let's be real. You thought I was going to let you marry someone I haven't fully vetted? I spent at least four hours this week looking through his grandmother's second cousin's best friend's social media. And I can attest to the fact that your future hubby is a complete hottie."

"Okay, great. You caught me. He's definitely attractive, but it doesn't matter. We're just friends, and this wedding isn't even real. It's just a year of our lives and then we part ways on good terms," I remind her, leading Duke toward the door and waiting for Avery to follow me out.

"Yeah, I'm sure that's exactly how it's gonna go," Avery mutters skeptically, pulling the door to our apartment closed behind her. "But with that, we're officially out of here."

"I guess so. I know this isn't what we planned, but I'm kinda excited to spend the summer at the beach again," I admit as we make our way to the parking lot.

"Same. I mean we may be broke bitches for the foreseeable future, but as sad as we are about losing our teaching jobs, I'm already less stressed knowing I don't have to step back into a classroom for at least a year."

I nod in agreement, knowing exactly what she means. "Yeah, here's to trading grading papers for helping hotel guests," I say as we make it to our cars. After opening the door and letting Duke into his spot in the back seat, I turn back to my best friend.

"Let's do this."

"ALL RIGHT, Duke, we've made it to our new home," I tell him, pulling into the parking lot of the High Tide Hideaway. I'm embarrassed by how long it's been since I was here. As I got older and busier with school, Memaw insisted on coming to Smith's Valley to visit, and when her health started to decline four months ago, I moved her to the local assisted living facility so I could check in on her. Within a month she was gone, and she'd demanded that we cremate her and save the "fuss" of a funeral. I never intended to spend this many years away from a place that was so special to me, but as I look at the Hideaway, I realize I might have more work cut out for me than I originally thought. The once vibrant pink siding is patchy and spots are almost white thanks to sun damage, and the bushes and plants out front are overgrown and wilting.

Reaching over to pull out my phone, I send a quick text to Wyatt.

> Stella: Hey! We just made it to the Hideaway. Let me know when you want to go over logistics for tomorrow.

> Wyatt: Sounds good. I have one more tour for today, but as soon as they're over, my brother and I will come by to help you unload.

> Stella: That sounds good, but you don't have to help us. Pretty sure I'm never gonna repay you for all you're doing for me as it is.

> Wyatt: This isn't a competition, Stella. We'll be over there in a few hours.

> Stella: Sounds good. Avery's dying to see the town so we'll probably walk around while we wait.

After pressing send, I look back at the backseat where Duke spent the ride napping. He perks his head up at me, and his tail knocks against the side of the door.

"You ready buddy? Come on, let's go see our new home," I tell him, getting out of the car and opening the back door to let him out.

Avery throws open her door from where she pulled up beside me, and yells, "Oh my god, I can't believe we're here!"

"Yeah, we made it," I tell her, leading us toward the main entrance.

"Wait, so I totally should have asked this already, but do you know who's been keeping everything running since your Memaw passed?" Avery asks, and I shrug.

"Not really. When I called Mr. Marshall on Tuesday to tell him the plan, he said the place has kinda been in limbo for the last few months. I think there might be a few people here, but I really don't know what to expect," I admit, stopping to let Duke sniff the bushes beside the door. "I'm so damn nervous."

"I know, but whatever it is, we'll figure it out," Avery says. "Let's do this, Stels."

She opens the door for me, and I take a deep breath before stepping inside the lobby. I smile at the sight of the bright pastel interior where I spent all my childhood summers and breathe in the familiar scent of the sea breeze mixed with the vanilla air freshener my grandmother always loved.

Tears prickle my eyes, longing for her to come sweeping out of the small office behind the counter to kiss me on the cheek like she used to. Blinking them back, I turn to my best friend. "Well, welcome to the Hideaway."

"It's really cute," Avery tells me, looking around. "But, uh, are we the only two people here?"

"Um, I'm not really sure," I admit. "Hello, is anyone here?" I call a little louder, waiting to see if anyone emerges from the office.

"I mean the door was open, so surely there's someone around here," Avery says, turning in circles.

"Yeah, I mean I know the hotel's technically mine, but is it weird that I still kinda feel like we're trespassing?" I ask, and Avery giggles.

"We're definitely not trespassing, but I know what you mean. Come on, you can give me a tour, and hopefully we'll run into someone."

"Okay that sounds g—" I start just as I hear an excited shriek behind me.

"Oh my god, Stella, is that finally you?"

I turn to see Miss Clara, one of my grandmother's best friends, hobbling toward me. She's gotta be in her eighties and she hobbles over to me on her cane.

"Hi, Miss Clara. How are you doing?" I ask, trying to figure out what's going on.

"I'm a whole lot better now that you're here, darling. We've been waiting for you to show up for months," she says, almost knocking me over as she hugs me and hits me in the back with her cane.

"Wait, what? Have you been running this place, Miss Clara?" I ask, looking around.

"Well, that might be a bit of an exaggeration, but I guess you could call it that. I promised your grandmother I'd keep the lights on and the doors open until you showed up, but I never imagined it'd take this long," she chastises me. "Don't you know you're not supposed to keep an old lady waiting?"

"Oh goodness, I'm so sorry, Miss Clara. I don't know why Memaw told you that, but I didn't know anything about this whole situation until earlier this week. Last I heard, she was thinking about selling the place."

"That old hag was always sprouting out the most ridiculous things, wasn't she?" Miss Clara says with a wave of her hand. "Well, anyway, you're here now, and that's what matters. And you have the cutest little dog too," she points out, bending down to pet Duke who's sitting at my feet. "But wait, who are you?" she asks, turning to Avery.

"I'm Avery, Stella's best friend. I moved down here to help her with the hotel," Avery explains, reaching out her hand to shake Miss Clara's. "It's nice to meet you."

"Nice to meet you too, darling," Miss Clara responds, taking her outstretched hand and pulling Avery into a hug. "I'm glad she has help. I'm afraid, with the state of things right now, she's going to need it."

"Oh, that's comforting to hear," I say with a nervous laugh.

"Well, now that you're here, come on over and let me show you the books," Miss Clara says, reaching out and taking my hand to pull me over to the counter. To be so old and on a cane, she's surprisingly fast, and I have to hurry to keep up with her.

"Okay, here we are," she says, grabbing a bright pink book off the side of the check-in counter. "So, all of the bookings for the summer are recorded in the front. And then in the back, there's a list of monthly expenses and the staff members we're currently employing. And in this little lock box down here is all the hotel room keys and a few extra master keys for the stock rooms."

"Thank you, Miss Clara. Do you know how many guests we currently have?"

"Oh, dear, maybe one or two? Definitely not more than three."

I blink at her in surprise. "Wait, that's it? I knew we were down on reservations, but there's over fifty rooms in this place. And it's the summer season," I say, feeling my panic start to rise. I hadn't expected much, but I didn't expect it to be this bad. "What about the pool and the restaurant?"

"Honey, your grandmother closed down the restaurant almost two years ago. It's turned into a storage room for right now. But the pool is open if any of the few guests we have want to use it."

"Wait, really? I can't believe she left all of this out of our conversations," I admit, and Avery pats my back in comfort.

"It'll be fine, babes," she tells me before we turn back to Miss Clara. "Thank you for keeping everything going in the meantime, Miss Clara. How have y'all been handling bookings here? Are there any websites, social media logins, or anything like that we should know about?"

"Oh, darling. The High Tide Hideaway doesn't have any of that new-fashioned tech stuff. There isn't a website. All of our reservations are done over the phone."

Avery and I both pause, waiting for her to tell us that she's joking, but she just shrugs. "It worked for your grandmother for years, so she never saw any need to go through the trouble."

"So wait, how do guests find out about this place?" Avery asks.

"I don't know. Most of the people that I've seen come through here have been coming here for years. But like I said, I've just been standing in as a favor to your grandmother since she passed, so I don't know enough to help you there. But enough of all this talk, I've got an hour until I have to meet the girls for bingo. Now that you're here, I'm going to leave you with it. Good luck, darling," Miss Clara says, hugging me again and leaning over to pet Duke's head before heading out the door.

I look over at Avery, and I see the same look of shock on

her face that I'm sure is on mine. "Uh, so this might be a much bigger undertaking than we planned," I tell her.

"Yeah, you're right, but we're gonna make it work," Avery reassures me. "Let's find me a room and figure out where I'll be living."

"That we can do," I say before looking down at the mostly empty list of guests. "The good news is I'm pretty sure we have plenty of options."

"Hell yeah." Avery laughs, pointing at a random room number. "Let's go with this one for now."

"Perfect. Let me finish showing you around and then we can walk around town while we wait on the guys if we have time. Wyatt's brothers and a friend offered to help us move our stuff in when they get off work, but I'm not exactly sure what time that'll be."

"Hell yeah! We don't have to move all our shit by ourselves this time? See, if you ask me, there are some real perks to this whole marriage gig."

CHAPTER 9
WYATT

"Okay, I think that's everything for the day. Are you ready to go see your new wifey?" Trent asks me as we finish rinsing off the boats for the last time today.

"God, you're having way too much fun with this," I groan.

"Hell yeah, I am." Trent laughs. "If it was anyone else, I don't know that I'd think too much about it. But since it's you? This whole situation is too damn good not to have some fun with."

"Sure, whatever. Let's just go get them moved in. There's so much shit I need to take care of before tomorrow evening, and I don't have time to deal with you," I grumble, stepping off the boat and starting to walk down the pier.

"You know, as your newly ordained favorite brother, I don't appreciate the way you're talking to me," Trent jokes.

"Yeah, yeah. I already told you thank you," I say defensively.

"Yeah, I can feel the gratitude radiating off you as we speak."

"Whatever. Are you ready to go?" I ask as we walk into the office to grab our keys and shut down everything for the day.

"Sure. I just need to answer a couple emails and make sure the schedule for tomorrow is finalized. You go ahead and I'll meet you over at the hotel in a few minutes," he answers, and I wave at him before heading out to my truck.

> Wyatt: Hey, I'm done for the day and am about to head over. Are y'all around?

> Stella: Yeah, we're here. We'll meet you in the lobby.

> Wyatt: Sounds good. I'll see you then.

It only takes a few minutes to make the short drive over to the High Tide Hideaway, and as I pull into the parking lot my throat tightens with nerves. With the business of the last few days, I haven't had time to give the whole situation too much thought, but now that I'm here, it hits me that I'm really doing this. I don't regret making the suggestion to Stella that we get married, and I stand by the idea that it doesn't have to mean anything serious between the two of us. But at the same time, I've never done anything this impulsive in my life.

Taking a deep breath, I make my way inside and see Stella and another girl, who I'm assuming is the friend she told me about, sitting together on the sofa in the corner.

"Hey, Stella," I say, and she looks up to smile at me.

"Oh my god, he's even hotter in person," her friend says loudly, and Stella bumps her with her leg to silence her.

"Hey, Wyatt," Stella says, walking over to give me a hug. "This is my best friend, Avery. Avery, this is Wyatt."

"Nice to meet you," I say to Avery, who smiles at me.

"Likewise. I've heard a lot about you these last few days, but I'm happy to put a face with the name," she says, causing Stella to roll her eyes.

"Okay, enough of that," Stella interrupts.

Before she can say anything else, a dog emerges from under the coffee table, dragging his leash on the ground and running over to where we're standing.

"Uh, I'm hoping this is your dog?" I ask, looking down at the lab at our feet.

"Yep. This is Duke, and he's the best boy," Stella answers, her eyes widening. "Oh my god, I just realized I never even told you I had a dog. I hope that's okay."

I nod, bending over to pet the pup. "Yeah, that's totally fine. I've always loved dogs."

"Oh my god, do you remember the time one of the guests brought their dog and it escaped from their room? Pretty sure we spent the entire day looking for him, and we found him asleep in the linen closet buried under all the towels?" Stella asks with a laugh.

"Yeah, I got the little guy out and he spent the rest of the trip escaping out of his room to find me because I gave him all those treats," I respond, chuckling at the memory.

"All right, I hate to break up the walk down memory lane, but we've got a shit ton of stuff to move and a wedding to plan," Avery points out.

"You're right. Why don't we talk about tomorrow while we wait on the rest of the moving crew to get here?" I suggest.

"That sounds perfect," Stella agrees, and we move to sit on the couch.

"Before we get too far into this, I just have to make sure, are you sure you're still good with this whole situation? I still can't believe we're doing this," she starts, and I hold up my hand to interrupt her.

"Stella, I told you that I promise I'm good with it. Remember, one year with no strings, and then the hotel's yours," I tell her.

"Hell yeah it is," Avery interjects.

"Okay, as for tomorrow, I figured we could do the ceremony on the docks after I finish my tours for the day. It's private enough so maybe we can keep the rest of the town from sticking their damn noses in our business. I took care of the marriage license and my brother also got ordained yesterday so he's good to go."

"Damn, Wyatt, you've kinda already taken care of everything," Stella says.

"It really wasn't a big deal. A quick visit to the county clerk and that was it."

"Well, still, I'm grateful," she tells me just as the front door of the lobby opens and Everett, Bennett, and Trent come in the front door.

"Moving crew's here," Bennett yells as he walks in the door.

The three of us stand and make our way over, and Trent's the first to speak. "There she is. Hey, Stella. Long time no see," he says, reaching out to hug her. "Are you sure about marrying this grumpy old fella?"

"Hey, Trent. I know it's been a long time. And oh yeah, I'm sure." She laughs, before turning to Everett. "And hi, Everett. It's good to see you again too."

Everett nods in acknowledgment. "Yeah, I was happy to hear you're moving back."

"Yeah, this wasn't exactly how I saw my year going, but I'm honestly pretty excited about taking over the hotel."

Bennett steps forward and reaches his hand out toward her. "Hey, I think we met a time or two years ago, but I'm Bennett, Wyatt's best friend."

"Yes, I remember. Nice to see you again. And this is Avery, my best friend," Stella says, gesturing to where the tall blonde is standing. "Oh, and the pup's name is Duke."

My brothers and best friend all bend down to greet the dog before Avery asks, "Damn, what the hell do they put in the water down here? Does everyone in Crestbrook look like this?"

"Avery," Stella yells, covering her face with her hands.

"What? I'm just speaking the truth." Avery shrugs, looking unapologetic.

Everett, Bennett, and Trent all laugh at her outburst and I shake my head at them. "Okay, let's get their shit moved in. Avery, which room are you in?"

"I'm in Room 112 down here on the first floor. I'll show you where my car is parked. I really appreciate y'all coming over to help us," Avery answers, walking toward the door.

"Sounds good. And Stella, you're in the cottage off the back, right?" Trent asks.

"Yeah, I haven't even been back there yet. We got caught up checking out the hotel. Let me go find the key in the stash by the front desk. Y'all can help Avery in the meantime. Wyatt, you're waiting to move everything this weekend, right?"

"Yeah, with work and everything this week, I haven't had time to pack everything. But since my apartment's just down the street, I can knock it out in a few trips later."

"Sounds good. Let's get to it," Bennett says, following Avery out to her car.

As they filter out of the lobby, Stella and I walk over to the counter and open the lockbox where the keys are. Duke follows us and lies at our feet while we start sorting through the stack.

"Oh my god, this is such a mess," Stella says with a sigh. "When we grabbed Avery's key, it was sitting on the top, so I assumed it wouldn't be too hard to find. But I'm starting to think I couldn't have been more wrong."

"It's going to be fine. We'll find it," I tell her, looking at the box Stella's digging through. "Let me look through there."

She moves out of the way, and I catch a whiff of her coconut and vanilla perfume before gesturing for me to take over the search. Sitting down in front of the box, I start checking the numbered keychains for a few minutes before realizing she was right.

"Jesus, when was the last time this was organized?" I mutter, and Stella laughs.

"Knowing my grandmother, probably at least ten years ago. She wasn't particularly known for her organization skills."

"I can see that. Let's see—315, 204, 213, 215, 316, linen closet, 314, 115, pool cabana…" I mutter, reading out the key numbers as I sit them aside. "Wait, here it is," I say triumphantly, holding out the key labeled "cottage."

"Oh, thank god." She sighs, reaching out to take it from my hand. "Want to go see our home for the next year?"

"Sure, let's do it," I tell her, letting her lead the way out of the side door toward the pool. Glancing around, it hits me that there aren't any guests around. I know tourism is down around here, but it feels weird to be walking around a completely empty hotel. "Don't take this the wrong way, but, uh, are there any guests around here?"

She laughs uncomfortably, looking around the patio. "I

don't really think so. Maybe a couple? I've gotta sit down with the reservation book tonight and try to figure that out, to be honest. Apparently, Miss Clara's been managing everything since my grandmother passed, and I think this might be a bit of a bigger undertaking than I originally thought."

"I'm sure it'll be fine," I assure her, following her down the small path to the cottage near the back of the property.

"Yeah, I'm sure you're—" she starts, coming to an abrupt stop on the narrow path in front of me. I barely have time to stop in front of her, reaching out to steady both of us while Duke barks happily at our feet.

"Oh my god, this place is going to need so much work," she exclaims, looking at the overgrown vines snaking their way up the house.

I resist the urge to cringe as I notice the cracked window on the side of the house but I just shrug. "No big deal. I'm sure the inside is still in good shape. Let's see what we're working with in there."

She nods and unlocks the door, pushing it open and stepping back. "No offense, but I'm gonna let you go first if you don't mind."

"Don't tell me you're afraid, Stella," I tease, walking inside and taking in the living room and kitchen. "See, all good, There's absolutely nothing to worry about."

"Okay, fine. I'm sorry I'm being a baby. And you're right. The inside really doesn't look that—" She starts letting Duke inside, walking toward the bedroom door, and opening it before letting out an ear-splintering scream.

I run over, trying to figure out what the hell's wrong. Behind us, Duke barks loudly at the outburst. Pushing her aside, I look inside the door frame. "Wait, what's wrong?" I ask, eyes wide at the scene in front of me. The room is completely empty other than the bed and a dresser in the corner, but I'm pretty sure that's not what she freaked out about.

"In the corner!" she cries, causing me to look further into the room.

"Oh, holy shit," I mutter, seeing what she's talking about. I don't know how she spotted it so quickly, but there's a huge lizard coiled in the corner closest to the door. "Um, how the fuck did a lizard get in the house?"

"That's a great fucking question!" she yells, clearly beside herself with panic. "Wait, wait, wait. Why the hell are you walking toward him?"

Ignoring her, I step further into the room and closer to the green lizard coiled up in the corner of the room. He's gotta be almost a foot long, and I cringe as I notice how sharp his claws look even from across the room. He lets out a low hiss, and Stella screams again.

"Whoa, it's okay. I'm almost certain he's harmless. He doesn't look poisonous," I reassure her, trying to find something positive about the situation.

"I don't give a shit what kind of lizard he is," she cries, holding her leg out to stop Duke from coming inside. "Duke, my sweet boy, you cannot go in there."

"It'll be fine. Just keep Duke out of the room while I go find a shovel from outside and then I'll take care of the lizard."

"You can't kill him," she yells, and I look at her in surprise.

"Wait, so you don't want me to kill him?" I ask, trying to figure out what she's asking for.

"No. I don't want him in here, but he can't help that he ended up in the wrong place. And I absolutely cannot handle lizard guts all over the floor. Plus, he'd be kinda cute if he wasn't in my damn bedroom. If we open the window, can you scoop him up and throw him out or something?" she asks, petting Duke's head as he continues to bark.

"Uh, yeah, I guess I can do that," I say, looking down at the reptile. "Do you happen to know where a shovel might be around this place?"

"Not a clue. I know she used to keep some gardening stuff in the back shed around here. Other than that, your guess is as good as mine."

"Let me go look. Give me a second," I say, rubbing my face with my hands and walking out to the small shed beside the cottage. After searching for a moment, I find a decent sized garden shovel and head back inside.

I find Stella and Duke huddled in the doorway, watching the lizard with wide eyes. "Okay, let's get this taken care of."

Stella nods at me and says, "God, I owe you for this one. There's no way in hell I could have taken care of this by myself."

"Sure," I tell her, opening the window and turning back to the lizard. "Come on, little guy. I'm not gonna hurt you but I need you to let me move you. You can't stay here."

He hisses at me as I move closer and Stella lets out a tiny scream.

"Hey, hey. It's fine," I reassure her, taking the shovel and scooping the lizard up.

He continues to hiss at me, and as I move toward the window, the lizard starts to climb up the wooden base of the shovel toward me.

"Oh my god," Stella yells. "Just throw the whole damn thing out the window."

Deciding she's right, I throw the lizard and the shovel outside where it lands with a clunk and the reptile scampers off into the trees around the cottage.

I look down at Stella and see Duke looking back and forth between me and the open window, his eyes wide in surprise.

"Wyatt, is this really how we're starting our marriage?" she says, her eyes wide. "This has to be the worst omen in the history of the world."

I can't help but laugh at her outburst. "It's fine. I think it's just a sign that this year is going to be a big adventure."

"I guess you're right. But holy shit, I just thought about it. What if there's more? I'll never be able to sleep in this place."

"It'll be fine. We'll get your stuff moved in and then you can stay in the hotel tonight. We'll call an exterminator tomorrow to make sure there aren't any openings or holes where critters can get in."

"Okay, good point. I need to calm down. I swear I'm not usually this much of a disaster," she says nervously. "This week has just been a lot."

"No worries. Now, are you ready to head back? The guys will never let me hear the end of it if they think I brought them over here to work and ran out on them."

CHAPTER 10
STELLA

"Are you ready to do this?" Avery asks me the next afternoon as she helps me put the finishing touches on my makeup.

"Yeah. Ready or not, right?" I ask with a laugh, fluffing my hair. "Are you sure this dress is the right move?

"Absolutely," she reassures me, looking down at the short white dress I found in the back of my closet. "You look beautiful, babes."

"Thank you, Aves. I don't know what I'd do without you," I admit.

"Of course. I seriously can't believe you're getting married today."

"Me either, honestly," I admit and we both laugh. "All right, I guess we'd better go ahead and head that way."

Avery nods, and we head out to her car to make the short drive over to the docks. "Will it just be us and the guys who we were with last night?" she asks as I give her directions.

"Yeah, I mean I'm not expecting anyone else. We both know this isn't a real wedding so I don't see any reason for anyone else to com—" I start but stop as I see the full parking lot of the dock.

"Uh, are you sure about that?" Avery asks, looking out at the crowds of people setting up lawn chairs on the dock. "Oh my god, did you know there were going to be flowers? And twinkle lights?"

I stare in shock at the scene in front of us. "Um, I'm pretty much at a loss for words."

"Same," Avery admits. "Let's go see what this is all about."

We walk toward the hut labeled as Crestbrook Charter Company, and every couple of feet, someone stops me to congratulate me on the wedding.

"Stels, what the hell is going on?" Avery asks me with wide eyes.

"Not a fucking clue," I admit, smiling at the people around me. "I mean, I remember a few of these people from when I spent the summer here, but I've never seen a lot of them before in my life."

"Do you think Wyatt did all of this?" she asks, and I shrug.

"I mean, surely not. I know he said he was going to handle putting everything together, but we never talked about inviting anyone."

As soon as we step foot into the small office space, Wyatt runs over, clearly aggravated.

"Hey, you look nice," he says before gesturing to the crowd. "I'm so sorry about all of this. Fucking Miss Agatha and her inability to mind her own business."

"I'm confused. Who's Miss Agatha and what does she have to do with all the people outside?"

Wyatt sighs. "She's the town busybody, and she runs the local newspaper, *The Cove Column*. Somehow she found out about the wedding, and she put an invitation in the fucking newspaper without telling me. And some of the ladies in town heard that we weren't planning to decorate, and they took it upon themselves to decorate while I was out on my last charter."

Avery burst into laughter beside me. "Oh my god, living in this fucking town is gonna be a hoot."

"Okay, so now that they're here, what are we going to do about it?" I ask as I look out the window at the people continuing to pile out of their cars. "And how much weight can this dock hold? Because there's at least a hundred people out there."

"God, I don't wanna deal with this shit today. But okay, this is what we're gonna do. There's no way we're getting rid of them now that they know what's going on. But we can tell them they have to sit on the shore. I'm sure none of them came with a microphone or anything like that, so there's no way they'll be able to hear us. It'll be like they aren't even there," Wyatt suggests, and Avery nods in agreement.

"Honestly, I think that makes sense, Stels. I don't see any way out of it, so this seems like the best scenario for now," she says and I have to admit she's right. "I'll leave you two to talk for a moment, and I'll start redirecting people."

"Good luck," Wyatt says with a laugh. "Trent should be out there in the chaos somewhere. Get him to help you."

"Not a problem," Avery says, leaving the two of us to stare at each other.

I laugh at the absurdity of the whole situation.

"Oh my god, this whole thing just keeps getting more and more out of control. Do they know this marriage isn't even real?"

He shakes his head. "Listen, Stella. I don't think it's a

good idea to broadcast that. The more gossip we give them, the more obsessed with us they'll be."

"So we just pretend like we're madly in love?" I ask with a laugh, but I stop when he shrugs.

"It's up to you, but I don't think you remember how over the top they can be. Do you want to spend the next year explaining all of this over and over again? Our friends already know the truth and in my opinion, that's all that matters."

I think about it for a moment and realize he might have a point. "Okay fine, but Wyatt, wait, oh my god. We're gonna have to kiss. For the first time. In front of the entire population of Crestbrook Cove."

I feel my panic start to rise again and Wyatt reaches out and puts his arm around me. "Hey, calm down. It's just a kiss. It'll be fine."

"I guess you're right," I say hesitantly and he looks at me, clearly realizing that my latest revelation is affecting me more than it probably should.

"Wait, Stella, this is really bothering you now, isn't it?" he asks, and I shrug.

"I know it shouldn't. I think it's just really hitting me that all of this is actually happening. And now everyone's gonna be watching and it'll be weird."

"It's okay. You know, there is a really easy solution to this problem?" he says, and I wait for him to elaborate.

"Why don't we just have our first kiss now?"

I blink at him, waiting for him to laugh, but when he doesn't, I realize it's not the worst idea I've ever heard. "Wait, is it weird that I don't hate that idea? Not because I'm dying to make out with you or anything. I know this whole marriage thing is just a friendship thing, but what if we don't and we go to kiss during the ceremony and everyone can tell it's the first time? Or we could—" I'm rambling and before I can finish, Wyatt leans down and drops a gentle kiss on my mouth.

I freeze, completely taken aback before my mind finally catches up to what's going on and I relax into the kiss. I get lost in the kiss for a brief moment and all I can think about is how good his mouth feels on mine. It probably doesn't last more than twenty seconds, but when we both pull back I can't help but feel a little off-kilter before focusing on giving myself a mental pep talk. *It's not anything romantic, Stella. You just haven't kissed a guy in years. It doesn't mean anything.*

"Not too bad, huh?" Wyatt teases, and I can't help but laugh.

"No, I think we're good on that front," I admit before looking out at the now empty dock. "I guess Avery and Trent managed to get everyone moved out of the way."

"Yep, so I guess that's our cue. Are you ready to get married?"

"Let's do this thing, hubby."

"LAST CHANCE TO make a run for it," Avery teases, as music starts playing on the deck from a sound system one of the locals showed up with a few minutes ago. Clearly this town is way more prepared for my wedding than I am.

"Nope, I'm good. Plus, I don't think I'd get very far even if I wanted to. There's probably three hundred people out there, Aves," I point out, and Avery grimaces.

"Yeah, they just kinda kept showing up didn't they? I can't believe one of them brought microphones so they could hear the ceremony from the shore too. I can't believe how fast they pulled all of this together."

"Me either," I admit before taking a deep breath and saying, "okay, I think it's time. I'll be right behind you."

"Perfect. I know this isn't a real wedding, but you look gorgeous as a bride, Stels."

I smile at her as she walks out of the small office. I take a moment to steady myself before grabbing the small bouquet Miss Clara brought me and follow her down the makeshift aisle.

I can tell the shore is stacked with people, but I try to ignore it, forcing myself to look straight ahead to where Avery, Wyatt, Bennett, Trent, and Everett are waiting for me at the end of the dock.

After what feels like forever, I'm close enough for Wyatt to reach out and take my hand, and I can almost feel my body sag in relief. I've never been someone that wants all the atten- tion on myself, and all of the eyes behind us are enough to have me feeling on edge already.

"Good afternoon, everyone, you may be seated," Trent says. Even with my back to the crowd, I hear the shuffle of hundreds of people sitting down in their lawn chairs.

"We're gathered here today to celebrate the marriage between Stella Hale and Wyatt Robinson." Trent starts, and I zone out for a moment as he welcomes everyone.

After a few minutes, he says, "If anyone has any objec- tions to this marriage, speak now or forever hold your peace."

I freeze when I hear yelling behind us. I swear, if some ex- girlfriend showed up to stop him from marrying me, I'm going to lose my mind. This is my only shot at keeping the hotel, and now that I'm back, I can't imagine it in anyone else's hands.

I turn, expecting to see a woman our age making her way down the pier, but instead I see one of the older ladies waving her cane around in protest.

"Fucking hell, Miss Eleanor," Wyatt mutters under his breath, and I give him a strange look.

"She's one of Miss Clara's friends from the knitting club. She's the biggest flirt I've ever met, and apparently she has a little crush on me that she won't let go," Wyatt explains, and I look back at the lady to make sure we're talking about the same person.

"Wyatt, that woman has to be ninety years old," I tell him, my eyes wide.

"Yep. She's harmless, but this is a bit much for me," he admits just as Miss Clara walks over and uses her cane to push Miss Eleanor back into her chair.

"You may proceed," she yells as loudly as she can from the shore before sitting back down in her own chair and picking up what looks like a knitting project.

Trent looks between us, waiting for directions about what to do until Wyatt whispers, "Let's get this thing going again, huh?"

"Right, sorry. It's time for vows. Wyatt, you're first," Trent tells us, reading off the paper in his hands.

I'm only half listening as Wyatt recites his vows, overwhelmed with how fast this is all happening. After a moment, Wyatt squeezes my hand and whispers, "It's your turn, Stella."

I shake my head, realizing I completely zoned out during my own wedding before giving Trent and Wyatt a warm smile. "I got distracted. I'm so sorry, but could you repeat what you just said."

"No problem. Let's try this again. Stella, please repeat

after me," Trent says, as he starts reciting the traditional vows again from a paper in front of him.

"I, Stella Hale, take you, Wyatt Robinson, to be my lawfully wedded husband," I say, trying to focus on keeping my voice steady as I repeat the rest of the vows.

As soon as I finish, Trent turns to Wyatt. "Do you have the rings?"

I look around in panic, realizing ring shopping never occurred to me over the last week. "Here you go, I've got 'em both," Wyatt says, and I look at him in surprise.

God, this man really thought of everything. What kind of wife am I making him buy his own wedding ring? I think, breathing a sigh of relief as he pulls both rings out of his pocket.

It doesn't take long for us to exchange rings, and before I know it, Trent gestures to us. "I now pronounce you husband and wife. Wyatt, you may now kiss your bride."

Wyatt smiles and reaches out, cupping my face before leaning down and kissing me gently. The kiss only lasts a few seconds, but I feel myself melting into him the same way I did when he kissed me in the hut.

He pulls back and whispers, "You were right, Stella. I'm glad we practiced."

I laugh at that just as Trent turns to the shore full of people and yells, "I now present to you Mr. and Mrs. Wyatt Robinson."

The crowd screams and cheers, and Wyatt grabs my hand to lead me back down the dock. Despite the fact that we didn't plan for everyone to find out about the wedding, I have to admit that the decorations they set up are beautiful. There are orange and white flowers on all of the posts that perfectly match the sunset behind us, and the lights twinkle off the water.

"God, can you believe we're married?" I whisper as we walk back down the makeshift aisle.

"Yeah, I know we're doing this as friends, but I wasn't expecting it to feel that damn real."

"Same," I admit. "Here's to a year of friendship and married bliss, am I right?"

"Hell yeah. It's wild how much can change in a week, huh?" he says and I can't help but laugh.

"God, has it really only been a week?" I sigh. "I feel like the last few days have been such a whirlwind. In the last few weeks I lost my job, moved to a new state, inherited a hotel, married my childhood friend, and walked into a fucking lizard living in my bedroom."

"Damn, well, when you put it like that…" he says. "But despite how crazy everything's been, I think we're making the best of this whole situation. And I'm glad you ended up back in town."

"Yeah, I always loved spending the summers here," I admit as the crowd of locals heads toward us.

"Are you still feeling that way?" Wyatt whispers, taking in the mass of people heading our way. "Because at this exact moment, I'm kinda wondering why I haven't gotten the hell out."

"Come on, they're harmless. And I'm pretty sure they won't ever leave us alone if we don't acknowledge them," I say, and he gives me a look just as Miss Clara hobbles over as quickly as she can.

"Hey, there. You know, when I saw the announcement in the paper this morning, I didn't think it was real. I figured there was no way you wouldn't have mentioned it yesterday, and I've gotta say, my feelings were hurt. But then I remembered what it was like to be young and in love. We could barely keep our clothes on, so I'll give you a pass this time."

"Oh, um, thank you for that," I tell her, and Wyatt shoots me a look over the top of her head.

"All right, well, on that note, we have a lot of people to see, but yeah, we'll see you later," I tell her, pulling Wyatt away before she can say anything else.

"One down, at least a hundred and fifty-seven to go," I murmur to him, and he groans.

"Fucking wonderful."

CHAPTER 11
WYATT

"God, I don't think I've ever been so happy to see the Hideaway in my life," I murmur when we pull up in front of the hotel. It took us over an hour to make it back to the car after talking to everyone who showed up to our impromptu wedding ceremony and then we met up with my brothers and Avery at The Sand Bar for dinner.

"Same," Stella agrees. "I ended up having a really good night once we got through all the awkward small talk after the wedding. But at the same time, I thought it was kinda sweet how excited they were for us. It kinda made me feel like an asshole for lying to them."

"You know, I thought about that, and the way I see it, we're not really lying. We really did get married today, and that's all they need to know."

"Yeah, I guess you're right. Well, are you ready for our first night in the cottage? I still cannot believe I'm actually planning to stay there after the lizard incident from hell," Stella teases, shaking her head with a laugh as she gets out of the car.

All night, I've tried to ignore how beautiful she looks in the white dress she picked for the ceremony, and as she turns to look back at me under the glow of the street lights, I remind myself for the hundredth time that we're just friends.

"Oh, I'm sure it'll be fine," I say, grabbing the small overnight bag I packed for tonight and following her through the empty lobby as we make our way back to the cottage. "I talked to the exterminator after he came by today, and he said we should be good to go. He sealed all the holes he found where he thought they might be coming in, and I already called someone to work on the cracked and broken windows too. They should be here tomorrow."

"God, I feel absolutely useless," she groans before adding, "but seriously, I don't know what I would've done without you, Wyatt. I don't know how I'll ever thank you."

"Don't mention it. I know this might come as a shock given how well I handled our little friend yesterday, but I was not particularly stoked by the idea of waking up next to anything with scales," I admit, and she freezes, halfway through unlocking the front door.

"Wyatt, stop! Don't even joke about that," she yells, and I try not to laugh at the look of disgust on her face. "Oh my gosh, I'm never gonna sleep in this place."

"I'm kidding, Stels. It'll all be fine," I promise her, pushing open the door and bending down to pet Duke as he runs toward us.

"Wait, did you just call me Stels?" she asks, closing the front door and sitting crossed-legged to let her dog crawl in her lap. "It's been years since you called me that. You, Memaw, and Avery are the only people who I've ever heard use that name."

I pause, realizing how easily her old nickname fell from my lips. Shrugging, I fidget with the bag in my hand. "Well, I figured since we're married, it would be fine. But would you rather I didn't?"

"No, no. It's totally fine. It just caught me off guard," she says, shooting me a small smile as she turns to her dog and nuzzles her face into his fur. "Duke, did you have a good afternoon? Go get your ball and we'll play."

The dog darts off toward Stella's bedroom we set up yesterday, almost knocking me over as he runs past me in excitement, before running back into the room with a bright blue ball and dropping it on her legs.

She giggles, and his tail knocks against the floor, waiting for her to throw it. "I know, buddy. Go get it."

Duke races around the room, chasing the ball, and Stella looks back at me. "So, Avery and I spent a few hours today fixing up the guest room for you. I know you've still gotta move all your stuff over, but hopefully, it'll be enough to get you by for tonight."

"Oh, you didn't have to do that. But thanks. I talked to my landlord and I just need to have everything out by the end of the week. So I've got about a few days to get everything taken care of."

"After everything you've already done, it was the least I could do," she says, rising from where she was sitting on the floor.

"No problem, Stels. But I've got a tour early in the morning, so I'd better get to bed," I tell her.

"Oh, of course. Sorry, this whole thing kept you out so late. But uh, good night, Wyatt."

The two of us stand there for a moment, and for the first time I feel a bit of the awkwardness of the situation we're in finally sinking in. As of today, I'm married to Stella, but this marriage looks so different than anything I ever expected. Am I supposed to hug her? Kiss her on the forehead? Ask her what her plans are for tomorrow? Or, are we supposed to pretend like the other person isn't here unless there's a problem with the hotel?

God, this is ridiculous, I think to myself, breaking the silence and reaching out to pull her into a hug. "Good night, Stella. Here's to lizard-free dreams."

She gasps, pulls herself out of my embrace, and knocks me in the arm. "God, you're such an asshole. I'd almost forgotten about all of that. But good night, Wyatt. Do you want me to plan dinner for us tomorrow night?"

"Sure, but don't feel like you need to cook. We can order out or whatever you want. We don't have many tours so I'll be back pretty early, so we can talk a little more about how we want to drum up some business around here."

"That sounds good. I'll see you then. Night," she tells me before looking down and turning her attention to Duke. "Come on my sweet boy. Let's go to bed."

She leans in and hugs me again, and I take a moment, feeling the last bit of awkwardness I was feeling between us fade away as I soak in the scent of her coconut and vanilla perfume. "Thank you again, Wyatt. I'm really grateful for you," she whispers, pulling back and turning to lead her dog into her bedroom. And I'm left in the hallway wondering what the hell I've gotten myself into.

Damn, it's too early for this shit.

That's all I can think of as I walk up to the *Fin and Tonic* and see that someone tied hundreds of helium balloons to the rails. They range from a mix of wedding rings and cake designs, all of them with *JUST MARRIED* written across them in bright sparkly letters. There's also a huge sign hanging across the front that features a caricature drawing of Stella and me with hearts in our eyes.

"Damn, now that's the way to celebrate a wedding," my brother yells behind me, and I turn, flipping him off as he gets closer.

"Can you remind me why the hell I stayed in this goddamn town?" I grunt, before throwing up my hands in frustration. "What the hell am I supposed to do with all this shit?"

"Uh, that's a great question, but it's too fucking funny to be upset about," Trent says, continuing to laugh at my expression.

"Seriously, Trent. On top of being really annoying, this is just so damn wasteful. Plus, they touched the *Fin and Tonic*," I grumble, walking over and starting to rip at the strings tethering the closest balloon. After it's untied, I stab it with the knife I keep on board, shaking my head at the pop it makes as it deflates. "Are you gonna get your ass over here and help me or am I doing this shit by myself?"

"Chill, dude. I'm coming."

Trent jumps over the railing and starts helping me pop the balloons before asking, "So, how are you feeling after last night? Don't think I didn't notice that you and Stella looked pretty happy at The Sand Bar last night."

"I'm fine. And you know that Stella and I always had fun together. Don't try to make this into a big deal, cause I'm not in the mood."

"Big deal? Wyatt, you're fucking married. You, *the marriage isn't ever gonna be for me* brother, volunteered to marry a girl you haven't seen in a decade. And you expect me not to notice that you look happier than I've seen you in years? I call bullshit."

I scowl at him, and he holds his hands up in surrender. "Fine, fine. I'll drop it. But don't think that Bennett, Everett, and I aren't keeping an eye on you."

"Well, that's nothing new. I love y'all but the three of you can be annoying as fuck," I tell him, and he chuckles while we continue taking down the balloons around the deck.

"Back at ya," he responds, looking down at the large sign hanging off the boat. "Damn, someone really put some serious detail into this thing."

"Just take the fucking thing down. We have a tour in thirty minutes, and we've gotta get all this shit gone."

Trent shakes his head at me. "No, we don't. I checked the email this morning and they canceled on us."

"Damn it. We're going to have to change our cancellation policy because this is the third time this month."

"Wyatt, we don't have any policy around here. Or a website. Or customers at the moment."

I glare at my brother and fight the urge to punch one of these damn balloons in frustration. "Wow, Trent. Thank you so much for the update. I surely haven't noticed that we've only done a quarter of the charters we had by this time last year. I don't know what I would do without you."

"Okay, sorry. You're right. We'll figure it out. Maybe with your wife revamping the Hideaway, we'll get some new tourists. But either way, we'll make it work. We always do," he reassures me.

"Yeah, I guess so. Anyway, since we apparently don't have any tours today, I'm volunteering you to come help me move my stuff into the cottage. Let's finish cleaning this shit up, and then we'll go."

CHAPTER 12
STELLA

"Okay, are we ready to start Operation High Tide?" Avery asks, collapsing onto the couch in the lobby.

"Yep, may as well get to it. This place isn't gonna fix itself," I tell her, rubbing the top of Duke's head as he lies in my lap.

"You're right. But also, before we get too far into this, I need to know how your first night as a married woman went?"

"Oh, obviously it was super eventful. We had a kinda awkward hug goodnight and then Duke and I went to the bed and spent a few hours cuddling until I finally fell asleep."

Avery shoots me a look of disgust and shakes her head at me. "Why the hell was it awkward? If you ask me, the two of you should just bang and get it over with. There's no way that it won't happen sometime in the next year, and the sooner you rip the Band-Aid off the more hot sex you get to have."

"Aves!" I yell, looking around the lobby to make sure no one's around. "For one, you can't talk like that out here! What if the guests hear you? And second of all, I've told you at least a hundred times in the last week that we're just friends. Nothing is ever going to happen between the two of us."

"Stels, I love you, but we'd have to have guests in order for them to overhear me. And fine, I believe you. But whenever it does happen, expect to hear I told you so," she teases. "On another note, I thought you said that there would be staff here at the hotel. I'm pretty sure Hotel Management 101 says we aren't supposed to just leave the lobby open like we did all day yesterday."

"Uh, yeah. I think that might be something we have to add to our ever-growing list of problems. Mr. Marshall told me some of the staff is still around, but all I've been able to figure out is that Miss Clara was running it basically solo while she waited for us to show up. There's a name for a housekeeper who comes once a week since we have so many uninhabited rooms, but that's about it," I say. "So it looks like it might be a two-woman show around here for a little while. Memaw left a little bit of money to go toward upkeep, but even with that amount, there's no way we can afford to pay full-time staff members right now. I'm pretty sure we have exactly two guests right now."

"Yeah, you're right but that's fine. Neither of us has ever minded a little bit of hard work," Avery reassures me, pulling her pink laptop out of the bag at her feet. "I was having trouble sleeping last night, so I started to put together some ideas for a new logo and a social media strategy. This place definitely needs a little bit of upkeep, but I think with some new paint and a great website, we could really turn this place around."

"I think that's a good plan. Can I see the logo ideas?" I ask, leaning over to look at her computer screen. Duke blows out a sigh of annoyance as I shift under him, and I pat his head in apology.

"Okay, obviously these are just some rough sketches, so if you hate them we can trash them and try again. But what do you think?" she asks, turning her screen in my direction so I can see it.

My mouth drops open, and I stare at the computer in shock. "Aves! You did all this last night?"

On the screen, there are at least five different logo options, a stockpile of at least ten social media posts, and some other fun doodles that we could incorporate with our branding.

"Yeah, but like I said, if you hate it, I can totally restart. I was just trying to get an idea of what you might like."

"They're freaking perfect, Aves. I've always known how talented you are, but this is wild. I love all of them," I say as I go through some of the pictures.

"Well, you know, it's amazing how much I can get accomplished now that I'm not managing a hundred and fifty kids every day. I loved teaching so much, but I wasn't expecting to feel this free, you know? I feel like all of my creativity is coming back now that I know I'm not going back to the classroom this fall."

I nod because I completely understand what she means. I've told myself for years that teaching was my calling and I had to be obsessed with it in order to be good at my job. And while I don't think I ever would have made the decision to leave on my own, I have to admit that it feels good not to worry about decorating my classroom or calling parents anytime in the foreseeable future.

"But enough about that," Avery continues, pulling me

from my thoughts. "Why don't we start with the new logos and you can tell me which one's calling your favorite. Once we have that, I'll use the colors and fonts to help design the website, and then maybe we can start taking reservations."

"Oh, it's so hard because I love them all," I tell her truthfully, pointing to the one that caught my eye first. It's a vintage hotel sign with a surfboard and a palm tree coming out of the top, and the pinks and blues match the hotel colors perfectly. "I think this one."

"Ah, okay, that one is my favorite too. I'll get it cleaned up and then start using this style to add to those posts I've started. And I'll work on setting up all of our social media accounts too and send you the login information too."

"All of that sounds perfect. Now we just have to figure out how to get people to come stay here."

"Yeah, I was thinking about that too. And I feel like we need to decide who our target audience is. Is it families looking for a quick getaway? A romantic couple's destination? Or a fun girls' trip? Obviously, we're probably going to get all of it once we hit our stride, but I think the clearer we can make our vision, the better chances we have of filling this place up."

I think about it for a moment before I ask, "What if we market it as a wedding and bachelorette location? The walk-up access to the beach and the outdoor bar beside the pool area would both be ideal for a small wedding. And I know when my friends from college got married we had the hardest time finding somewhere that could accommodate us all that wasn't crazy expensive."

"You know, that's not a bad idea. You and I could plan some events here at the hotel, and we could offer a catered dinner on the beach too. I feel like we could put together some packages, and I'm sure some local businesses would be willing to partner with us too. Maybe some boat tours from your new hunky hubby?"

"Yeah, I think that would be so fun. We could offer a welcome party at the pool and maybe some morning fitness classes too if any of the groups are interested," I suggest.

"Wait, Stels. I think this could actually work," Avery says. "Plus, weddings are more expensive than just the average hotel stay so that could be a good way to make some extra money. But they're also a ton of work. So why don't we try the girls' trip and bachelorette route until we feel comfortable hiring more staff, and then we can reassess after that? And we could always offer bachelor parties too, but honestly, we'd have to call in reinforcements from your hubby on that one. I have no idea how to plan a weekend for a whole group of dudes."

"That sounds perfect. Let me text Wyatt and see if he's willing to work with us on this," I tell her, pulling out my phone and sending him a quick message.

Stella: Hey, Avery and I are talking and we had an idea on how to drum up some business for the Hideaway. But I wanted to run it by you real quick if you don't mind because once I tell Avery to roll with it, there will be no going back.

Wyatt: Sure, go ahead.

Wyatt: Just don't leave me hanging because honestly your best friend scares me just a little bit.

I laugh at that, and Avery shoots me a suspicious look as I go back to typing.

Stella: We're thinking about building some packages for bachelorette trips and girls' weekends. What do you think about something where we offer slightly discounted rooms and boat tours if they're purchased together?

I see the dots pop up indicating that he's typing before they disappear again. That happens several more times until finally my phone rings and Wyatt's name flashes across the screen.

"Hey, so I'm guessing the phone call is your way of letting me down easy, huh? If you don't want to do it, that's totally fine. There wasn't meant to be any pressure. I'm so sorry if it made you feel unc—" I ramble until Wyatt takes pity on me and cuts me off.

"Whoa, Stels. It's fine. I'm not calling you because I'm upset. I feel like this is something we can make work. But just to be clear, most of these rides aren't fishing trips, right?" he asks.

I cringe, knowing he probably won't love the answer I'm about to give him. "No, probably not. Think more of a booze-cruise type of thing."

Wyatt groans on the other end of the line, and I hear Trent in the background trying to convince him to just give it a shot.

"That's what I thought. Well, it's not exactly how I wanted to get our business out of the hole, but we've gotta do something. So I'm good with it. Let's try it," he finally says, and I hear Trent whooping in the background.

"Are you sure?" I question, wanting to make sure he's really good with this.

"Yeah, I'm sure. Am I super excited about the idea of

driving some drunk girls around all summer? Absofucking-lutely not. But we all need the money and the business so I do think this could be a decent solution," he says, still not sounding overly happy about the idea. "But I do have a condition."

"Oh, okay, sure. Of course. Whatever it is, we'll make it happen." I rush to explain. I have no idea what he's going to ask for, but I'm sure it'll be a small price to pay to make this work.

"You and Avery have to agree to come on any of these trips that we do. Let's be honest, they're going to want to take thirty-seven thousand group pictures, and I'll be so done by the end of it that I'll probably throw their phones in the water. So, if you promise to come help entertain them, we're all in."

I try not to burst out laughing when I hear Trent in the background cheering at the answer Wyatt just gave me, but finally, I can't help it and start giggling.

"All right, that's fine. I can live with that," I say as Avery dances a little in her seat beside me. "Okay, well, we're gonna get back to work over here, but thanks for saying yes. Are y'all in between charters right now?"

Wyatt sighs in frustration. "Actually no, we're done for today. All the rides we had booked canceled on us, so Trent and I are at my apartment trying to get all of my shit packed. I should be back to the Hideaway in a few hours."

"That sounds good. No rush," I tell him. "I guess Duke and I will see you then."

"Sounds good," Wyatt says. "Good luck with all the planning."

"Thanks, we'll probably need it," I murmur before hanging up the phone and meeting Avery's gaze. "Uh, he said yes."

"I heard. And I saw the way your smile got about ten

times bigger when he did. You still want to pretend like nothing's going to happen between the two of you over the next year?"

"Yep, because it's not," I promise her. "Now, let's plan some dream vacations, huh?"

CHAPTER 13
WYATT

"How's married life treating you?" Bennett asks as I slide into a booth at The Sand Bar.

Stella and I have been married a few weeks now, and we've settled into a pretty great routine. Basically, it feels like I have my old best friend back. We work our respective jobs during the day, and then usually spend the afternoon working on the hotel. We've managed to repaint most of the rooms in our free time. We also brought in a company to refresh the pink exterior paint, and we've done a decent amount of work to upkeep the flowers and trees around the pool. But despite launching the website and social media campaign almost two weeks ago, they've yet to get any bookings through the new system.

I shrug and murmur, "Fine. She and Avery are meeting us here in a little bit. They were waiting for their one guest to check out so they could close everything down."

"Shit, man, that's rough. I sure would love for business to pick up around here. The shop has been completely dead for weeks. If we can't drum up some business, I don't know what we're going to do," Bennett tells me.

"Yeah. Same here. Shit absolutely sucks. But hopefully, we'll get some momentum heading into the Fourth of July. That's always our busiest week of the year."

"I thought so too, but you saw how slim the crowds were for Memorial Day."

"I guess you're right," I mumble.

Bennett looks over the glass of his beer and eyes me suspiciously. "Man, what's going on with you?"

"Nothing," I insist. "Just stressed about work."

"Are you sure that's it? Because I've said at least ten things that would normally have you completely pissed since we met up earlier this afternoon, and you haven't responded to any of them. Don't get me wrong, I'm a fan of this more mellow Wyatt, but I've never seen you act like this. So what is it? Are you and Stella fighting or something?"

"No, we're not fucking fighting. Can we just fucking drop it please?" I growl and he holds his hands up in surrender.

"Okay, I'll take it back. I knew that same old grumpy asshole was in there somewhere," Bennett says with a laugh just as Avery and Stella appear behind the booth we're sitting in.

"Hey, Stels." I reach out to pull her into the booth next to me and kiss her forehead. I tell myself I do it because half the town is currently in here for dinner, but there's a small part of me that wonders if that's really all there is to it. I've come to terms with the fact that I'm definitely more than a little attracted to Stella, but I've promised myself I would never try anything, at least until after the year's deadline has passed. I would never forgive myself if she ever felt forced into anything with me, and with the current setup of our relationship, I don't want her to feel like she has to do anything with me as a thank you for helping her out. I know she thinks that spending this year married to her was a huge inconvenience, but really, it's the happiest I've been in a long time.

"Hey, y'all. Sorry to keep you all waiting. We had a late checkout, and it took a little bit longer than usual," Stella apologizes.

"Don't worry about it," Bennett tells her, and Avery slides into the booth next to him.

"Oh my god, I'm starving," Avery groans. "And I've been dreaming about that pineapple vodka lemonade since lunchtime.

"Ugh, same," Stella groans. "I don't know what the hell your brother puts in those things, but they're so damn good. Have y'all ordered? I don't mind going to the bar and putting our drink orders in if that's easier."

"Yeah, we grabbed some beers when we came in, but I don't mind getting you and Avery whatever you want," I offer, and Stella shakes her head.

"Nope, I got it. I'll be right back," she says, bouncing off to the bar where my brother's working.

"So, how was today at the Hideaway?" Bennett asks Avery, causing her to go into detail about the new ways she's trying to get the hotel's name out there. I zone out for a minute and turn when I hear a squeal over by the bar next to where Stella is standing.

"Oh my god, Stella, is that you?" a girl calls from across the bar, but there are too many people in between for me to tell who it is.

Avery and I both crane our necks to look for whoever yelled at Stella, and finally, after a moment I see Chloe Hill emerging from the crowd of locals who just came in the door and running to give my wife a hug.

"Who's that?" Avery asks me, looking over at the two of them.

"Chloe Hill. She supervises the lifeguards for all of Crestbrook Cove, and she and Stella used to be great friends when she visited, but I don't know if they kept in touch," I admit, watching as Stella grabs her drinks and leads Chloe over to our table.

"Oh my god, I could not believe it when I heard you were back in town! It shouldn't have surprised me when I heard you married this guy but I just can't believe how fast it happened. I was gone for a few weeks attending some training, and I heard you were back and married in the time I'd been gone," Chloe rambles as Stella gestures for me to scoot further into the booth so Chloe can sit with us.

I do as she asks, trying to act like I'm annoyed, but I'm mostly excited to have an excuse to have her so close to me. Sure enough, as she slides into the booth, she presses her small body against mine, and I wrap my arm around her to pull her close.

"Gosh, if you two aren't just the cutest thing," Chloe says with a giggle as Stella hands Avery her lemonade.

"Thanks, babes," Avery tells her before Stella pauses to introduce the two of them.

"Avery, this is Chloe. Chloe, meet Avery. Avery and I have been roommates for the last several years, and she moved down here with me to help me take over the Hideaway. And Chloe and I were great friends when I spent my summers down this way. I'm so glad we finally ran into each other. I thought about you the other day and I was thinking you must have moved away from Crestbrook Cove since I hadn't seen you yet. But I'm so happy to know I was wrong."

Chloe and Avery smile politely at each other from across the table, and Stella keeps babbling away excitedly.

"We have to have a girls' night or something soon. I know there's not a ton of options in Crestbrook, but I bet we could still come up with something really fun to do together."

"I'm totally in," Avery agrees. "We've been working so hard on the hotel. I feel like we still haven't done a very good job of exploring the town. I've lived here for almost three weeks now, and I still haven't been to the beach!"

"Oh yes, that would be so much fun! I'd absolutely love —" she starts but is cut off when Avery checks her phone and squeals loud enough that the whole restaurant turns to look at us.

"We just got our first booking!" she yells. "Five rooms and the bachelorette package!"

Stella screams at the announcement and jumps over Chloe to get out of the booth and hug her best friend. Bennett and I shake our heads as they jump around excitedly.

"Wait, when is it?" Stella asks, her eyes wide.

Avery pauses, reaching across the table for her phone. "God, I was so excited we finally got something, I didn't even think to check. Let me look."

She taps away at her phone for a second before she looks up, and I realize she looks slightly pale.

"Uh, well they check in the day after tomorrow," she says, looking at Stella. "Shit, how the hell are we going to pull this off? That's literally less than forty-eight hours until they're here, and we still have so much to do at the Hideaway before it's ready."

"Great question, but we're just gonna have to make it work," Stella says.

Before the girls can say anything else, Chloe interjects. "Hey, it'll be great. I have the day off tomorrow, so I'm happy to come help."

"Yeah, Stels. I don't think we have but one charter

tomorrow so you can put Trent and me to work too," I tell her.

Bennett nods in agreement. "Yeah, I should be able to slip away from the shop tomorrow afternoon too. We'll make it work."

"God, I love living in this town," Avery whispers to Stella, causing her to giggle.

"Yeah, I don't mind it either," Stella agrees. "Let's drink up and get something to eat, so we can head back. We have a weekend to plan."

CHAPTER 14
STELLA

"I don't think I've ever been this excited or exhausted in my whole life," Avery mutters the following night as we make our way out to the pool.

I nod in agreement, unable to believe how much we accomplished in the last twelve hours. When I woke up this morning, I walked over to the hotel to find at least twenty people who'd heard about our time crunch and showed up to help. Even Miss Agatha and Miss Clara made an appearance. Granted, they probably spent more time telling us what we should do rather than helping, but I have to admit it was still a really sweet gesture. After everyone showed up to help us today, we decided to use tonight as a test run for the first welcome party tomorrow, and most of the volunteers stayed to celebrate the fact that we're fully prepared for tomorrow.

"Yeah, same. But I think using the pool party as a thank you and a trial run for tomorrow is a genius idea," I tell her, and she smiles in acknowledgment.

"Thanks, I thought it would be a good way to make sure we're actually ready. I'm sure we'll still have some hiccups when they get here, but I think we'll both feel more comfortable with seeing how this is gonna go," Avery says, grabbing the stack of pizzas we had delivered from The Sand Bar and carrying them outside.

For the first time this summer, the pool is full of people—all of them swimming, drinking, and laying across the inflatable floats Wyatt and the boys spent an hour blowing up this afternoon. The boys also helped me thread lights around the corners of the pool patio, casting everything in a soft glow as the sun starts to set.

"Oh my god, seeing Miss Clara in a tiny purple bikini was not on my list of things to do today," Avery says with a laugh. "But also, if I make it to her age, I'll probably rock one of them too."

We both giggle at that, before heading off in separate directions to make sure everyone is having a good time. As I start to pass the pool, Miss Clara waves me over.

"Hey, dear. How are you feeling about tomorrow? Everything's looking so good. But don't forget if you need someone to come down and show you young ladies how to party, I'm more than happy to help."

"Oh, I really appreciate that, Miss Clara. But you've already been so helpful around here I couldn't possibly ask you to do that."

"Well, my offer still stands. Just let me know," she says before pulling an inner tube over her head and starting to float around the pool.

"Yes, ma'am, thank you," I say and continue my walk around the pool. I stop and make small talk with some of the locals along the way until Chloe walks up and threads her arm through mine.

"Come walk with me for a minute, girl. We didn't get nearly long enough to talk last night, and I'm so curious about you and your new hubby," she whispers, pulling me off to the side.

"It's been good. I know it's a bit fast, but it all worked out. Enough about me, though—I want to know more about you. Obviously, it's been a long time since we've seen each other so what's been going on," I deflect, not knowing exactly what to say about Wyatt and I.

"Oh, you know, nothing exciting ever really happens in Crestbook Cove. I'm still painfully single and spend most of my time working. We are majorly lacking in husband material around here, but it's fine. And most of my friends from high school moved away and never looked back, so I have to admit I'm really excited that you and Avery are here. I hope I'm not being too pushy, but I've been dying for some girlfriends."

"Trust me, we know that feeling. Why did no one tell me that making friends as an adult can really suck sometimes? We'd love to hang out with you," I tell her truthfully. It may have been a long time since we hung out, but Chloe was always kind to me during my summers here, and I remember we had a lot of fun playing games at the pier and gossiping about boys over ice cream as we got older.

"Sounds good. Why don't we plan to do a beach day next week? That way you can relax for a few hours after all the work you've put into the hotel these last few weeks."

"Let me talk to Avery, but that sounds like a great idea. It seems basically criminal that we've been here almost a month and we've yet to spend the day down there. Here, let me give you my number, and we can text to finalize the plan."

"Perfect. Thanks, Stella. Is there anything else I can do tonight? Everything looks great out here."

"Nope, honestly I feel pretty good about how everything's

going. But we couldn't have done it without everyone's help. I just can't believe we pulled it together this fast," I admit.

"You should be so proud. All of us know how much this place meant to your grandparents and I know they'd be so excited about all of this," Chloe says, pulling me into a quick hug. "Okay, I'm going to let you get back to it, but I'm so glad we got to chat for a little bit. I'll plan to see you next week."

"That sounds perfect. Thanks again, Chloe," I say, before continuing my path around the pool. I stop to make small talk a few times until I see Wyatt walking back from the direction of the cottage.

"Hey, everything okay?" I ask, walking over to meet him. We're a little shaded by the tree-lined path, but the lights from the pool are still bright enough to cast everything around us in a warm yellow glow. "I just realized it's getting kind of late, so if you want me to shut this thing down, just let me know."

"No, no. I just went to feed Duke. I knew you've been tied up here most of the day, so I just wanted to check on him for you."

I stare at him for a second and without thinking, I reach out to wrap him in a hug. "You're the absolute best. I headed that way twice earlier this evening and got totally side-tracked. Thank you so much for taking care of him"

I've told myself that I didn't have any feelings for Wyatt over the last few days, but as I stare at him in the moonlight, I know that's a lie. I've gotten used to taking care of myself over the last few years, and the way he's gone out of his way to make sure everything is taken care of is slowly chipping away at my heart.

"No problem," Wyatt responds, continuing to hug me. I resist the sudden urge to bury my nose in his chest and soak in the scent of the ocean and his sandalwood body wash.

He looks down and brushes a piece of hair out of my face, and on instinct I lean into his touch, bringing our bodies closer. "Stella, you're so freaking beautiful," he murmurs, leaning down, and I reach out, suddenly desperate to feel his mouth on mine.

He pauses, our mouths mere centimeters from each other, and I suck in a quiet breath, convinced that I'll combust if he doesn't kiss me.

"Wyatt—" I start to beg, shifting to close the distance, and our lips barely graze each other, just as I hear a high-pitched scream from the direction of the pool. Alarmed, I pull away from him, and we race back to the patio. There's a little more screaming, and several of the men are running in different directions. Most of the girls are huddling in the corner, standing on lounge chairs, and amidst the chaos Miss Clara is floating in the pool by herself.

"What the hell do you think happened?" I whisper, and Wyatt shrugs, clearly processing the best way to handle the shit show in front of us.

After a moment, Trent runs across the pool patio and yells, "Over here! I see him!"

Several of the other men race after him, and I notice Avery standing in a chair across the pool from us. "Come on," I tell Wyatt, marching over to my best friend. "Hey, Aves, what the hell is going on?"

Avery looks down at me and shakes her head. "God, Stels, it was such a mess. Apparently, a snake found its way onto one of the floats in the pool. We realized it when someone went to grab the float and accidentally picked up the snake instead. He managed to throw it without getting bit, but they're trying to find it now to make sure it wasn't poisonous. No one got a very good look at it in all the chaos. And as that was going on, y'all's little lizard friend made an appearance too. I thought you were exaggerating with how fucking big that thing was, but holy shit it was huge."

"God, we're definitely going to get a one-star review if this happens tomorrow," I groan and Avery lets out a short giggle. "Aves, I love you but I don't know what on earth you would find funny at the moment. This is going to be a disaster."

"I know I'm so sorry. It just hit me how different all of this is from our lives a few weeks ago. But we'll make this work. The men are going to make sure we're as reptile-free as possible, and other than that everything tonight went great," she says, and I have to admit she's right.

"Okay, you're right. I'm nervous about tomorrow, but I'm also so excited, you know? I know it's just one booking, but I'm really starting to believe we can do this," I admit.

"Because we can, babes!" she agrees, stepping down from her chair and pulling me into a hug to whisper in my ear. "And don't think I didn't notice you and your hunky hubby sneaking back from the woods a minute ago. I'm going to need every single detail tomorrow. I told you there's no way you'd make it a whole year."

"Nothing happened," I say too quickly, causing Avery to raise her eyebrow at me.

"Mm hmm. I love you, Stels, but we both know that's bullshit. That man looks at you like he's dying to devour you and I'm fucking here for it. Now, let's clean this stuff up, so you two can get back to whatever you were doing."

"Okay, I think we're ready," Avery says, looking around the lobby the next morning.

"Yep, I still kinda feel like I could throw up, but I think we've done everything we can," I tease, and we both laugh.

"Uh, same. I don't think I slept more than an hour or two last night. Every time I settled, I started thinking of things I needed to do this morning and before I knew it, it was time to get up."

"Ugh, same. I finally gave up around five this morning and went for a run through town," I tell her.

"Of course you did," Avery says, rolling her eyes at me. "Either way, I'm super grateful for strong coffee this morning, because without it I'm pretty sure I wouldn't be able to keep my eyes open right now."

"God, I still don't know how you drink that shit. It literally tastes like dirt."

"Yeah, yeah. I know how you feel about it. You stick to your runs and orange flavored energy drinks, and I'll drink my coffee in bed like a normal human," Avery teases, and I stick my tongue out at her.

"Are you sure you don't want to join me on my run tomorrow morning? We can go early enough that it shouldn't be too hot."

"Stels, I love you, but the last time you convinced me to go with you I thought I was going to pass out by the time we made it to mile two. And you made me keep going for five. There's no way in hell I'm making that mistake again."

"I told you I was sorry about that," I say defensively. "Plus, no matter what, you had to do two more to get home, so it made the most sense to just finish it."

"Yeah, I can feel how apologetic you are from here," she teases. "But I think…"

We both freeze at the sound of car doors opening and

closing outside. "Oh my god, they're here," I whisper, and Avery stares back at me with wide eyes.

"Where should we stand?" she mutters back. "We definitely should have practiced this!"

"Uh, let's both go behind the counter," I suggest, and we scamper across the lobby to stand behind the check-in desk.

We've both just managed to sit down when the door opens and a group of ten girls pile in.

They squeal at the sight of the pink lobby and the glasses of rosé we sat out for them, and Avery squeezes my hand under the desk.

"Good call on the welcome drinks, Stels," she whispers, just before the group turns our way.

"Hi, ladies. Welcome to the High Tide Hideaway Hotel. I'm Stella and this is Avery. We'll be taking care of you this weekend. We can get you all checked in when you're ready."

"Yes, that would be wonderful," one of the girls says, stepping closer to the check-in desk.

"I'm Penelope and I'm the maid of honor. I think everything should be under my name," she says, and Avery nods at her.

"Yep, we've got you all ready to go. And who's our bride?" she asks, turning back to the group.

A girl with long blonde hair steps forward. "That's me! I'm Mia. And oh my god, I was so excited when I came across your Instagram account and saw you had openings this weekend. We were supposed to go out of the country, but there was a last-minute issue with some of our passports so we had to pivot."

"Welcome, Mia. And yes! I'm so sorry to hear that, but I'm so glad that y'all were able to join us. We're here to help with anything you all may need during your stay. We have the basic itinerary that comes with the bachelorette package here but feel free to look over it and we can make any changes you'd like," I tell her with a smile, holding out the itineraries Avery and I made yesterday.

"Wait, this is incredible. Pool party, boat day, and dinner on the beach at sunset? This is going to be so much fun!" she squeals, and the other bridesmaids crowd around to look at the list.

"We're glad you're excited. But like Stella said, if there's anything you want us to change we'll be happy to accommodate that. I also have cards here where you can mark any food allergies or dietary restrictions. Just let us know if there's anything else we can do to make sure you all have the best stay possible," Avery adds, handing Penelope and Mia a small stack of the cards we printed right before the girls showed up.

"Nope, I think all of this sounds perfect. You two really made the maid of honor job a hell of a lot easier," Penelope teases.

"Wonderful, I'm glad we could help. As for your rooms, we upgraded the bride to our largest suite upstairs so you would have a sitting area if you want it, and we put the rest of you on either side," I say, reaching down and grabbing the keys I sat aside earlier this morning. "Y'all are in rooms 308, 310, 312, 314, and 316. The suite is 312."

"Perfect. Thank you both so much. You really thought of everything. I guess you're are used to doing these though, huh?"

Avery and I make quick eye contact and I have to fight the urge to giggle. "Actually, it's a long story, but we actually just took over the Hideaway earlier this month. You are our first bachelorette party, so please let us know if there's anything we can do to make your stay more comfortable," I say with a nervous smile.

"Oh my god, we're your first? Y'all are absolutely killing it so far," Penelope says, giving us a wide smile as she passes out the keys.

"You're too kind," I say, before addressing the rest of the group. "We'll give you all time to get settled and unpacked, and the pool party will be set up for you whenever you're ready. And Crestbrook Cove is pretty limited on food options for dinner but we can place an order from The Sand Bar nearby or y'all are obviously welcome to go out if you'd rather do that."

"Honestly after spending the last few hours traveling, takeout by the pool sounds like a perfect way to end the day. Do you have menus?" Mia asks, and Avery nods, pulling out the paper menus she collected from Everett yesterday.

"Perfect! Okay, ladies, let's get this party started!"

CHAPTER 15
WYATT

"How's it going?" I ask Stella while she runs around the pool area, making sure everything's set up for the first bachelorette event. "And what can I do?"

"We just got them checked in a little bit ago. I have a good feeling about this group, so I think it's going to be a fun weekend. I'm just making sure everything is ready for them when they come down," she answers, leaning down and grabbing a plastic pink tub from behind the bar. "But if you're offering, I'll let you take this inside and fill it with ice so I can finish the drinks they asked for."

"No problem, Stels. And really everything looks perfect," I say truthfully. Honestly, it's impressive how much she and Avery managed to liven this place up in the last few days. All of the plants around the pool have been manicured, making it so there's a clear view of the beach from anywhere around the patio. The small twinkle lights glow off the water, and the floats in the shape of wedding rings and pink flamingos are floating around the pool.

I make quick work of filling up the ice bucket, and as I

walk back to the pool I can't help but stare at Stella. She's talking animatedly to Avery so she's not paying any attention to me, and I take the moment to admire how hot my fake wife is. Her long brown hair frames her face perfectly, and the sundress she's wearing clings to her body in the June heat. I shake my head, determined not to let myself go down that road with her. We agreed we're just friends—and friends don't fantasize about kissing each other. And I'm pretty sure they don't fantasize about each other the way I did last night.

There was a moment in the woods yesterday when I was certain she wanted me to kiss her, but she hasn't acted any differently since our almost kiss, so I'm guessing I'm wrong. It makes me feel guilty knowing I finally gave in and jerked myself off in the shower at the thought of her after we got home last night. I've never come that hard in my life, but the knowledge of what I did has made me feel guilty all day. Really, we were both really clear on how we wanted this relationship to go, so what kind of creepy fake husband am I?

Pushing those thoughts from my head, I walk up to her with the ice bucket, causing Stella to smile at me. As soon as I set it down she wraps her arm around me in a hug. "You're the best, Wyatt," she tells me. I don't miss the way Avery watches us, suspicion heavy in her eyes.

"Okay, enough of this bullshit. You two may be okay living in delusion, but I'm not. When the hell are you two going to sleep together and get it over with? The tension between y'all is really some—" she starts, and I have to catch myself from laughing at her outburst as Stella leans over and covers Avery's mouth. Avery appears unfazed as she continues to babble incoherently around Stella's hand, and I just stare at them, trying to decide how I should react.

Thankfully I'm saved from saying anything as the guests

for the bachelorette party pile out onto the pool deck, squealing over the setup in front of them.

"Oh my god, this is so beautiful!" a girl, who I'm assuming is the bride since she's the only one wearing a white swimsuit, yells, and Stella and Avery just smile in acknowledgment.

Stella's hand left Avery's mouth as soon as the door opened, and although I know Avery won't bring it up in front of the guests, I can tell she's far from through with this conversation.

"Girls, do you see these floats? That wedding ring is seriously so cute. And more rosé? I'm in heaven," the bride continues. When I look over at my wife and her best friend, I can tell her praise means a lot to them.

"Okay, I need us to take lots of pictures before it gets too dark and our hair gets wet," another girl suggests, prompting the rest of the girls to drop their stuff and start lining up. "Stella or Avery, would one of you mind taking some group pictures?" she calls, and Avery immediately darts over and starts directing people on how to pose.

Stella and I make eye contact, and I know we're both thinking about the other night when we talked about her joining me for the boat charters for this exact reason.

"You were right," she whispers, and I can't help but smile at her.

"Yeah, I know," I tease, before adding, "but I think this is my cue to leave, so I'll go wait on the food at The Sand Bar."

"What, you don't want to stick around for the photo shoot?" she asks.

"I'm good, thanks. I know we just called everything in, so it'll probably be about an hour before I'm back."

"That sounds good, I'll see you then," she tells me, moving away from where we were standing and heading over to where the girls are taking pictures. I try not to stare too much as she walks away, but I completely fail.

Damn it, I'm fucked when it comes to this girl.

"So, y'all have a hotel full of women, huh?" Everett asks.

"Yep," I say, and he waits for me to continue.

When he realizes I'm not going to say anything else, he asks, "And how is that going?"

"Okay, I guess. I'm really proud of Stels and Avery, and the guests seem really impressed, mostly thanks to all the upgrades we've made in the last few weeks. But also, they take a lot of fucking pictures."

Everett bursts into laughter, shaking his head. "Okay, people on trips tend to do that, Wyatt."

"I know," I grumble, feeling my frustration rise the longer he talks to me.

"You know, it almost seems like you're annoyed at something else entirely, and you just don't want to admit it."

"Fuck off," I mutter, regardless of the fact that I know he's right. I'm starting to realize the more time I spend with Stella, the more I'm going to want her, even though I know I shouldn't.

"Fine, I'll drop it, but just know you're not fooling anyone around here. And the sooner the two of you admit it, the sooner you can stop storming around here like an asshole," he tells me before turning to the kitchen and coming back with several bags of food.

"Here's your food," he says, holding out the bags for me to take.

"Thanks, man. And I'm sorry. You're right. The last few weeks have been great, but it's also been a lot to process. I'm sorry I was a dick."

"Nothing new there," he mumbles, before turning and chuckling at his own joke.

"Yeah, yeah. Fine. Thanks for taking care of the food."

"No problem. See you later," he says, stepping back behind the bar to get back to work.

After loading everything up and making the short drive to the Hideaway, I grab the bags of food and make my way through the lobby and out to the pool. "Food's here ladies," I call out, and Stella and Avery rush over to grab the food from my hands.

"Perfect, thank you for picking this up for us," Stella says.

"No problem. Everything still okay over here?"

"Yep, we're going to feed them out here and then they're planning to go back to their rooms for a lingerie shower, so I shouldn't be out here too much longer.

"Okay, that sounds good. I'm gonna go check on Duke, but you can call me when you're ready to clean up. I'll come help you."

"You don't have to do that, Wyatt. But I appreciate it. I'll just see you at the house in a few hours. Give my sweet boy some cuddles in the meantime."

I roll my eyes at the suggestion, before saying, "Yep, sure. I'll be sure to get right on that."

Stella laughs, and I turn to head toward the cottage. Just as I'm almost on the path, one of the bridesmaids stops me.

"You must be her husband, huh?" she asks, and it takes me a moment to realize what she just asked me.

"Oh, yeah. I am. What gave it away?" I ask.

"You two look at each other the way my husband and I

do. I'd recognize the sight of two people in love anywhere. How long have you two been married?'

Holy shit. What is in the water in this damn town?

"Just a few weeks, actually," I answer, trying to ignore everything else she just said.

She smiles brightly, nodding her head. "Oh my, no wonder you two look so smitten. You two are still in your honeymoon phase. Congratulations."

'Thanks," I tell her, feeling more uncomfortable the longer I stand here.

"Sorry, I didn't mean to keep you. I'm a wedding planner and I just get so giddy watching couples like you. Love is such a beautiful thing," she says, hiccuping before reaching down to grab one of the seltzers I helped Stella ice down earlier and taking a long sip.

"All right, well, enjoy the rest of your night," I respond, before heading down the path to the cottage in an effort to get away from the turn our conversation had taken. Clearly, she doesn't know what the hell she's talking about, because Stella and I are just friends.

CHAPTER 16
WYATT

make it to the cottage and push open the door, looking forward to drinking a beer and relaxing on the couch until Stella comes home.

"Hey, Duke," I call out, looking around the room for him. "Come here, bud," I yell, trying not to panic.

I swear to god, if this dog managed to get out... I think just as Duke runs out of my bedroom.

"Oh thank fuck, Duke, I've been calling for you," I say in relief as I bend down to pet him. "Wait, why the hell are you wet?"

He looks at me, then turns and walks back toward my bathroom slowly, like he's waiting for me to follow him. "What the hell is going—" I start, but pause when I see the sight of my bedroom. Water is pouring out of the wall and there are at least several inches of water soaking into the carpet and trickling out into the hallway.

"Holy shit," I murmur. "Where the fuck is the shut-off valve in this damn place?"

Duke looks at me for a second before running over to play in the water shooting out of the wall.

"Damn it." I sigh, running back outside and looking for the valve to turn the water off, but it's so dark, it's almost impossible to find. After a few minutes of searching, I finally find it, twisting it as fast as I can to make sure the water is completely off.

"God, this damn cottage is going to be the death of me," I murmur, pulling out my phone. Before I text Stella, I text the local plumber, Bobby, and ask him to put us at the top of his schedule to fix the leak. After that's done, I also look up the number for a local restoration business and leave them a message asking them to call me back in the morning.

Deciding I can't put it off any longer, I open Stella's contact and type out a quick text. I would prefer not to bother her since I know how important this weekend is, but I know if she comes in and finds out I didn't tell her, she'll be super pissed at me.

Wyatt: Hey, so…I know you're still working, but I just wanted to let you know there was a minor incident at the cottage.

Wyatt: Don't panic.

Wyatt: I have everything under control.

Stella: The fact that you told me not to panic means I'm definitely VERY panicked.

Stella: What happened?

Wyatt: I promise it'll be fine.

Wyatt: The pipe in the bathroom burst. And it kinda flooded my bedroom.

Wyatt: And we won't have water for at least the next few hours.

Stella: …

Stella: Wyatt, I don't think you know the definition of MINOR!

Stella: Oh my god, what the hell are we going to do?

Wyatt: It'll be fine. I've already texted Bobby and I left a message with a restoration company to come help us get the water cleaned up.

Stella: Who the hell is Bobby?

Stella: New rule: when we're in the middle of a major incident, let's normalize using full names and titles please.

I laugh, remembering the similar conversation we had about Mr. Marshall a few weeks ago.

Wyatt: My bad. Bobby's the plumber in town. He was one of your grandfather's close friends, so I feel like he'll do everything he can to get us taken care of as soon as possible.

Stella: God, okay. I'll be there in a few minutes, but start moving your stuff that isn't soaked into my room. We'll figure out what to do with it when I get there.

Wyatt: I don't have to crash your room. I can stay on the couch until they're able to get everything fixed.

Stella: I'm not arguing over this, Wyatt. That couch is tiny. There's no way I'm letting you sleep on that thing when the only reason you're even in this situation is because of me. Plus, it's a king sized bed, so there's more than enough room.

Stella: As long as you don't mind sleeping in the same bed as me and my seventy-pound lap dog.

Wyatt: Wow, you're really selling this whole thing aren't you?

Wyatt: Just kidding. I don't mind at all as long as you're sure you're okay with it.

Stella: I'm sure.

Blowing out a breath, I walk back into the house and look for an old towel to start drying off Duke. Once I find one, I walk back into my flooded bedroom and find the dog exactly where I left him. He's staring at the wall like he's waiting for the water to start pouring out of the wall again any moment now, and I shake my head at his antics.

"Come here, buddy. Let's get you dried off before your momma shows up," I tell him, just as Stella walks into the room.

"Too late," she teases, before turning her attention to the room in front of us. "Oh my god, Wyatt, this is way more than a minor incident! This is going to take forever to get fixed."

"It'll be fine. Look on the bright side—at least it happened out here and not to some of the guests at the hotel right?"

Her eyes widen in alarm. "Holy shit, what if this does happen in the hotel?"

"I'm sure it won't, Stels. I know your grandparents had the pipes redone in the hotel pretty recently, and I'm sure the ones out here are just old. And if you're sure you don't mind having a roomie, then it really doesn't have to be a big deal."

I hear the words coming out of my mouth, but internally I know that's a lie. It feels like a major deal to put myself in this position when I can already feel my self-control slipping every time I'm around this girl. I promised her we'd spend the year as friends, and we're barely a month in, and I'm ready to throw all that to hell.

But despite how badly I want to push for more, I know I'll never forgive myself if she feels like I've taken advantage of her. I'm just going to have to suck it up and ignore whatever I'm feeling for her.

"No, I'm sure I don't mind. Honestly, can we just go to bed and deal with this tomorrow? I'm absolutely exhausted and I'm pretty certain the mess will still be here after a few hours of sleep."

"Yeah, that sounds like a good plan. I'll let you get changed, and I'll work on getting Duke dry."

"Thanks, Wyatt. Give me ten, and then you're welcome to come in whenever.".

"Sure, no problem. Now, come here, Duke," I say, shifting my attention to her lab at our feet. He's on his back rolling around in the water, and Stella lets out a chuckle.

"Yeah, you boys have fun with that. I'm officially at my limit of chaos with this place for today."

With that she leaves, and I look down at the lab still splashing at my feet and squat down so that I'm closer to his eye level.

"Okay, Duke, this is how this is gonna go. You're gonna stand up, and I'm gonna dry you off so we can get this shit over with. And then we're going to go to bed, and you're gonna stay between Stella and me all night to keep me from doing something really fucking stupid, okay?"

The dog blinks at me before running to the door and bringing back his ball, splashing my legs as he runs by.

"Great, good fucking talk, dude. We're not playing right now, but maybe when you're dry," I tell him, grabbing his collar to lead him gently into the hallway and closing the bedroom door behind us. "Okay, just be still. There you go. Give me your paw."

After a few minutes, I pause and make sure he's relatively dry and decide he's probably as good as he's going to get. "All right, you can go play now."

Duke immediately runs off to Stella's room, and I spend the next few minutes getting ready for bed. After I've procrastinated and reminded myself how bad of an idea this all is at least ten times, I blow out a breath and knock on the wall beside Stella's open door.

"Come on in," she calls.

"Hey, I think I managed to get Duke—" I cut myself off when I catch sight of her sitting on top of her covers in a tiny pair of shorts and tank top. Her brown hair is piled on the top of her head and I have the sudden urge to run my fingers through it. She looks so fucking sexy, and I focus on ignoring how turned on it makes me to see her like this.

God, what the fuck is wrong with me? It's not like I haven't spent the night with a woman before. Sure, it's been a few years since the dating pool in Crestbrook Cove isn't exactly overflowing with options. I've even been on a couple of casual dates that turned into more for a night or two in the past. But none of them have ever affected me the way that Stella is right now.

"Uh, yeah, I see that," she says, interrupting my thoughts, and I don't miss the shy smile on her face when I realize I never finished my previous statement. She gestures to where Duke is lying at her feet, but I was so wrapped up in the way she looked, I didn't even notice the seventy-pound dog lying in the bed. *Damn, I'm a hot fucking mess.*

"Oh, right. Well, are you sure you're okay with sharing a bed? I can walk up to the hotel and find a room if I need to," I offer and she shakes her head quickly.

"No, no. I'm sure. This bed is plenty big enough for the both of us, and I think I might be too much of a scaredy cat to stay in the cottage by myself. Plus, it's late, and there's no reason you should have to make the walk in the dark. Unless you'd feel more comfortable in the Hideaway?" She hesitates, fidgeting nervously with the blanket she's sitting on.

"Nope, I'm perfectly happy here," I promise her, making my way over to the other side of the bed and pulling back the covers. As soon as I sit in the bed and pull the covers over my lap, I'm flooded with Stella's scent, and I take a deep breath to remind myself one more time that we're just friends.

Shit, I'm so fucking gone for this girl, I realize, looking over at her as she rubs Duke's stomach.

Shaking my head to remind myself to behave, I ask her, "Did everything else go okay with the party tonight? It looked like they were having a great time."

"It went really well. I think they had fun, and they're really looking forward to going out on the boat tomorrow. I know it's our first group, but is it crazy for me to think that this could really work? If we can just get our name out there, we could really get the Hideaway on the map."

"It's not crazy at all," I tell her, fighting the urge to reach out and touch her. "You and Avery have worked so hard over the last few weeks, and I know you're just getting started with everything the two of you can pull off here. I'm really proud of you, Stels."

She looks at me, and she looks so vulnerable I feel like I'd do anything she asked me to at this moment. "Honestly? I'm proud of myself too. I feel like you may have figured it out by now, but I was diagnosed with anxiety in college after my parent's divorce, and between losing my Memaw and my teaching career, on top of everything that was going on here, I was really worried I'd spiral. I know it probably sounds silly, but I'm starting to believe in myself again."

"It's not silly, Stels. You've been through a lot the last few months, but you're making the most of it, and I think that's fucking incredible."

"Thanks, Wyatt. But let's be honest, none of this would have been possible without you. If you hadn't offered to marry me to pull this off, I wouldn't have had a choice in any of this. The Hideaway would probably be rubble on the ground by now, and you were right that night in my car. I don't think I ever would have forgiven myself. Between you and Avery, you two have helped me more than I ever could have imagined, and I'm just so damn grateful."

"I have faith that you would've made it work without me, but I'm not sad that I get to be the one to do this with you," I admit, before adding, "you know, I really missed you, Stels. I know you didn't owe me anything, but I hated it when you stopped visiting. It may be a little unconventional, but I'm happy you're back in Crestbrook Cove."

I catch a glimpse of her sad smile from the light of the candle by the bed and I force myself not to focus on how her mouth's felt against mine during the few quick kisses we've shared. "I know. I missed you too. Honestly, I missed this town and this quirky hotel. It seems so silly now that I've spent some time here, but after my parents divorced, I put off coming back here for so long. By the time I worked through all of those emotions, I was teaching and working nonstop in

Smith's Valley, and I didn't really have the time I needed to take care of myself, never mind driving down."

"I get that. You don't have to answer, but what exactly happened between your parents? I know I only saw them at the end of each summer when they came to stay for a few days, but I remember thinking they always seemed like they were obsessed with each other," I say, hoping I'm not crossing a line by asking.

"Yeah, they were until they weren't," she says simply. I think that's all she's going to say before she continues. "Let me start by saying that my parents aren't bad people. They met their freshman year in college and they were married five months after their first date. Then they had me before their first anniversary. Honestly, I think there were so many factors that went into it, but over time they just grew apart. They didn't ever fight, they just stopped caring. They told me they were getting divorced the day after my high school gradua- tion, and both of them were remarried and expecting babies with their new spouses before my twentieth birthday."

She goes quiet for a second before she says, "They gave me a good childhood, and they haven't ever been horrible to me or anything like that. But I think Memaw and I reminded them of their old lives when they were trying so hard to build these new families and there just wasn't room for us in their lives anymore. There was no falling out, we both just realized we were the only ones putting in any effort into the relation- ship. And eventually, they both quit answering the phone when we called. So Memaw and I figured it was us against the world. But this place is where I remember all of us being together. In my head, it reminded me of everything I felt like I lost for a long time…and Memaw didn't push me to come back."

I push down the sudden anger and frustration I feel

building in my chest as she talks, trying to figure out how in the world her parents could treat her this way. But I don't want to upset her so I just reach for her hand in the dark and say, "God, Stels, I had no idea. I'm so sorry they treated you that way, but I hope you know they're fucking idiots. And they're the ones missing out on a relationship with their daughter who is caring and funny and sweet and…" I trail off, and she squeezes my hand in acknowledgment.

"Thank you, Wyatt. I've come to terms with it over the years. When Memaw started going downhill, I reached out to my dad and he didn't even respond to my texts or voicemails. I understand starting over, but I can't imagine not caring if my mom was given only a few months to live."

"Fucking asshole," I mutter, unable to help myself, and Stella giggles.

"Yeah, pretty much what I thought too. God, I'm sorry, Wyatt. I just totally trauma-dumped on you. You're trapped in this bedroom with me because yours fucking flooded, and I can't stop talking about my family shit," she says, starting to pull her hand away from mine.

Unwilling to let her feel self-conscious about anything she just told me, I hold tighter to her hand and gently pull her arm so she has to slide closer to me. Once she's close enough to touch, I wrap my arm around her and she leans her head against the side of my shoulder.

"Stella, you told me because I asked about it. And honestly, I'm glad you did. But I just hope that you know that this whole thing says way more about them and their character than it says about you."

She laughs a little at that before she admits, "Yeah, that's what Memaw used to tell me too. Granted her language was a little more…colorful, but you get the idea."

"Imagine that?" I tease. "You know, your Memaw was one

of the sweetest ladies I've ever met, and I really loved her. Yet, at the same time, I don't know if I've ever met someone who could curse and throw insults around the way she did."

"God, I know that's the truth," Stella agrees. I feel her shift a little closer so that her legs press against the side of mine. "I just hope I'm making her proud, you know? I know there are so many things I'm probably screwing up, but I just can't bear the thought of disappointing her, even if she isn't here anymore."

"Stella, are you kidding? There's no fucking way she wouldn't be just as proud as I am of you. No matter what comes your way, you find a solution. Just think about the way the hotel's already got more bookings than it did when you took over. I just need you to realize how fucking incredible you are," I say, and she looks at me for a long moment before she leans up and kisses me hard.

CHAPTER 17
STELLA

don't know what comes over me, but as I listen to Wyatt say all of these incredibly sweet things to me, my control finally snaps and I can't keep myself from leaning over and kissing him.

As soon as our mouths crash, I let out a sigh of relief at the feeling of finally having his lips on mine. The last few days have been torture, and all I've been able to think about is having his body this close to me.

"Fucking finally," he groans before threading his hands through my hair and pulling my mouth back to his. I giggle in agreement, swinging my leg over him so I can straddle him, desperate to be as close to him as I can.

He runs his hands up my sides, and I shift gently, rocking against his hard cock until I cry out in surprise when I realize how large he is.

"Damn," I mutter, and Wyatt chuckles.

"You really know how to stroke my ego," he teases, pulling my mouth back to his. I continue to roll my hips against him and smile when I feel him start to harden beneath me.

"Baby, if you don't stop, I'm gonna come. It's been a long fucking time since I had a woman as sexy as you grinding on my cock, and I'm trying to behave here," he whispers. I smile at the idea.

Suddenly, I feel the small familiar swell of anxiety start to build inside of me at the thought of having sex with Wyatt. I've enjoyed sex in the past, but I tend to freeze up when it's time to actually go for it with someone new. I had a few selfish partners when I was in college, and I've been nervous about how long it can take me to orgasm ever since. Just as I'm about to spiral, Wyatt brushes a piece of hair out of my face, and I feel the wave of anxiety I was feeling lessen at the touch.

"Behaving is overrated," I murmur. Wyatt laughs, grabbing my hips to keep me still.

"Stels, shit, you're so damn hot," he groans, bringing his mouth back to mine and dropping another hard kiss to his mouth. "But I don't want us to rush into anything here. We have a whole year of living together, and I don't want you to feel like we have to do anything."

"I don't feel that way, Wyatt," I assure him. "I've just spent the last few days thinking about how good this would feel."

"Fuck, I can't think straight when you talk like that, Stels." he complains in between kisses. "But, I just want you to think about this. Make sure this is what you want, okay? Maybe we can keep it casual while we're married. Just friends who kiss sometimes, you know? But I want to make sure you know that none of this is expected. I'd never forgive myself if you felt like I took advantage of this situation we're in."

I pause, and after I push away the brief feeling of rejection

I realize that he's right. We can't afford to rush into this, and the last thing I want to do is mess up the friendship we've rekindled over the last few months, despite the fact that I'd love nothing more than to grind on his cock until he's ready to come right now.

"Okay, fine. I guess you have a point," I pout and Wyatt groans at my expression.

"Stels, don't make this any harder than it has to be. My self-control is already at pretty much zero."

"You're right," I say, dropping one more kiss to his mouth before crawling off of him and laying back in the bed. "I'm not trying to guilt trip you. We'll take this slow and see where it goes, deal?"

"Deal," he agrees.

"Great. Now let's get to bed. It's been a fucking day, and we have a booze cruise to lead tomorrow," I tell him, inflicting as much excitement as I can into my voice.

"Fucking fabulous," he groans, and I can't help but laugh at his lack of enthusiasm.

"Goodnight, hubby."

"Good morning, Stella. Do you want me to start a pot of coffee so it'll be ready for you when you get back from your run?" Wyatt asks, looking through the bedroom door from the kitchen as I'm getting out of bed the following morning.

I wrinkle my nose at him, and he laughs at my expression. "Sorry to be the bearer of bad news, but I cannot stand the taste of coffee. I'll stick to my orange cream flavored energy drinks."

"You don't like coffee at all?" he asks. I shake my head, slipping into the bathroom in my bedroom to get dressed for my run.

As soon as I'm dressed and my hair's in a high ponytail, I open the door to answer him. "Nope, I honestly wish I did. But now that you mention it, do you know where I can get a restock on my energy drinks here in town? For some reason the website told me it'll take them a few weeks to get here so I was just going to grab them from the store. I think I'm out after today."

"Uh, nope, I can't think of anywhere in town off the top of my head that will have them for sure but I can tell you the names of a few places you could call and ask."

"Sure, that would be great. I'm gonna go on my run but I'll be back soon."

I step outside and take a few minutes to stretch before I take off, heading down the path to the beach. I've been wanting to try warming up by running on the beach since we moved, and after the stress of the busted water pipe and the sexual tension between Wyatt and me from that kiss last night, I feel like this will be just what I need to get my mind off of everything.

Once I get to the beach, it takes me a while to warm up as I get used to the feeling of running with the sand beneath my feet. I push myself as hard as I can, waiting for the calm I usually feel while running to come. But today, it never does. For years, running has been my safe place where I can shut the world out and not have to focus on any of the things that are stressing me out. But today all I can think about is that kiss and the way Wyatt's mouth felt on mine.

You agreed you're just friends, Stella. That kiss wasn't friendly. He seemed fine with everything last night, but what if he was just being nice? And if he leaves because you pushed him too far you won't just lose him, you could lose the Hideaway too, my brain reminds me over and over again. God, why is this so damn complicated?

I know the safest thing is to make sure nothing like last night ever happens again. It makes the most sense for us to stay friendly and not cross any more lines until this year is over and he can walk away from this whole situation. But the thought of that makes my chest hurt. I never let myself acknowledge how much I missed Wyatt the first time I left Crestbrook Cove, too consumed with the drama of my parents' divorce and starting my first semester of college. But now? I realize not having him in my life might leave me feeling a little hollow. Not to mention the fact that when he kissed me back last night, it was the first time I've felt anything for a guy in years.

By the time I finish my run, I'm sweaty, sandy, and more confused than I was when I started. After making the short walk back to the cottage, I fix myself a glass of water and open the fridge, looking for my usual energy drinks. But all that's in there is coffee creamer and a few bottles of beer. Thinking back, I remember I drank the last one yesterday without realizing it.

Damn it, of all the days to not be caffeinated.

Blowing out an annoyed breath, I remind myself it's not a big deal and I can probably grab one of my drinks from a gas station on the way to the docks. I grab a quick shower and slide into a pair of jean shorts with a tank. It only takes me a few minutes to throw on some light makeup and brush my hair out so it can dry in the sun before I grab my bag and head out of the house. Pulling out my phone, I send a quick text to Avery to make sure she doesn't mind making sure the guests are taken care of.

Stella: I'm out of energy drinks. :(

Stella: If it's okay, I'm gonna leave now so I can run to the gas station and grab one. Can you make sure all the guests are good to go and I'll meet y'all at the docks? I want to make sure we have everything we need there too.

Avery: You and those damn drinks. You know this wouldn't be a problem if you'd just drink coffee like the rest of the world.

Avery: I'm just giving you a hard time. I'll take care of it. See you in an hour.

Stella: You're the best. Thanks, Aves.

Avery: Yeah, yeah. Tell me something I don't know. ;)

Rolling my eyes at her reply, I pull out of the parking lot of the High Tide Hideaway and head to the nearest gas station. I walk inside and smile at the older lady behind the cash register as I make my way to the drink coolers.

"Hey, honey. How can we help you today?" she calls out across the store, and I turn my attention back to her.

"Oh, I just came in to see if you had any energy drinks. Specifically the orange cream flavor, but I need some caffeine bad enough today I won't be picky," I say with a kind smile as the lady stares at me.

"No, dear. We don't carry anything like that. But we've got a hot pot of coffee over here if you want some of that. Cream and sugar too."

"Oh, that's okay. Thanks anyway," I say, trying to hide my disappointment as I head back outside.

I try three more gas stations, and by the time I pull up to

the docks, I'm frustrated and already looking forward to today being over. I knew there was a reason I said I never wanted to live in a town this small, and the current lack of caffeine options is currently at the top of the list.

Walking inside, I find Wyatt and Trent sitting around the desk and going through invoices. Looking up they both raise their hands in a wave of acknowledgment, and Wyatt says, "Hey, Stels. Perfect timing. This one here's about to give me a fucking migraine with the way he's running his mouth."

"Excuse me for wanting to make sure all the bills are paid. You've been a little more distracted than normal with every-thing going on the last month, and I just want to make sure there's nothing else I can do to help everything run smoothly around here," Trent says. I suddenly feel a sudden wave of guilt over all the time Wyatt's been spending at the Hideaway instead of here at work.

Wyatt must notice the look on my face because he holds his hand out at his brother to stop him from talking. "Stels, I can see that look on your face. My brother's being a dick but he didn't mean it that way. I'm a grown man and I've wanted to help you at the Hideaway. Plus, it's not like we've had a ton of business here anyway."

Trent's eyes widen as he looks at me. "Yeah wait, Stella. No one's upset with you at all. I was just giving him a hard time."

I nod at him and look at Wyatt. "For the record, not a damn place in this town has my drinks."

I know I'm being way grumpier than normal, but the combination of the lack of sleep and the lack of caffeine has me feeling more off-kilter than I'd like to admit.

"Damn, I was afraid of that. I'm sorry, Stels. Maybe you can find a way to get them shipped soon," he says.

"Maybe. So are y'all ready to get this party started?" I ask, determined to change the subject and get myself in a better mood.

"Hell yeah," Trent says with a wide grin on his face. "Getting paid to spend the day with a bunch of cute ladies seems like a pretty good way to spend the day."

"Dude, first of all, you have no idea what they look like. And second of all, I don't know why you think you're going. You've gotta stay here so you can take the other group that's coming in two hours. The bachelorette trip booked a four-hour charter so there's no way we'll be back in time."

Trent's smile falls, and he opens his mouth to argue before accepting defeat. "Fine, but the next time we have a bachelorette trip, I call taking them out," he says, crossing his arms over his chest.

"Uh, yeah, sure whatever," Wyatt mumbles, rolling his eyes before turning back to me. "Anyway, how much longer until they're here? I know the schedule says ten minutes, but I'm not sure if everything's running on time."

"Avery actually just texted me and said they're on their way, so it should be any minute now," I tell him.

"All right. I need to run outside and make sure the *Fin and Tonic* is ready to go. If you don't mind, I'll let you greet them and bring them up," he suggests.

"Sure, that's no problem. Go do whatever you need to do. I'll bring them up," I confirm, and he nods before heading outside to check on the boat.

I'm about to head outside when Trent stops me. "Hey, Stella. I know it's not really my place to say any of this and I know y'all's relationship didn't have the most conventional start, but I'm really glad you came back. I don't know if you've noticed, but Wyatt turned into a little bit of a grump over the last few years trying to manage everything for all of us. But he's not like that with you, and I'm starting to feel like he's going back to how he used to be. He'd kill me if he knew I was telling you all this, but I just wanted you to know I'm glad you came back."

I freeze, unsure of what to say and Trent just smiles at me. "Sorry, I didn't mean to make you uncomfortable. I just wanted you to know I've never seen him act the way he does with you with anyone else. And I know this whole thing started out fake, but just go easy on him, okay?"

"Uh, yeah. I care about Wyatt a lot," I admit. "I don't have any intention of hurting him, but I really appreciate what you're saying."

Trent waves, gesturing for me to go join his brother on the boat. "Okay, enough of that. Go have fun, and I'll take care of everything back here."

"Oh, right, I've gotta get going, but I'll see you later," I say, before heading outside to meet Avery and the rest of the girls.

As I wait for them, I feel a fresh wave of anxiety rise in my chest at what Trent just told me. I know he meant it as a compliment, but how in the world am I supposed to keep myself from falling for him when people say things like that?

God, how did this become such a mess?

"Is it just me or is this going really well?" Avery whispers, and I nod in response. We've been out on the water for a little over an hour, and like she said, things seem to be going even better than we planned.

"Uh, that's what I was thinking too, but we can't jinx it," I whisper, looking out at the front of the boat where the girls are lounging around, tanning, and drinking while '90s country blasts through the boat's speakers.

"I think they've got everything they need, and Wyatt looks like he's good to go," Avery says, gesturing to where Wyatt's maneuvering the boat through the water with the ghost of a smile on his face. "Why don't we go sit in the back for a little bit? We've been so busy with the hotel these last few days, but I need updates on my new favorite married couple."

I shoot her a glare and she laughs, grabbing my hand, and leading me to the back of the boat.

"Come on, we can go sit back here for a little while before we check on them again in a bit. There shouldn't be anyone back—" she starts but she comes to a sudden stop when we round the corner and see one of the bridesmaids sitting back here alone.

I vaguely recognize her from yesterday, but she was so quiet in comparison to all of her loud and vivacious friends that I didn't notice she wasn't with the rest of the group.

"Hi," I say, smiling at her. "Are you okay? Is there anything I can get you?"

"No, no. I'm so sorry I'm in the way. Let me move right now," she starts, sounding a little panicked.

"Oh my goodness, no. You don't have to move. We just didn't realize there was anyone sitting back here. But you're more than welcome to stay."

"I'm so sorry," she says again, starting to stand, but I hold up my hand to stop her.

"Please, just sit. What's your name?" I ask, trying to make her feel comfortable.

"I'm Hailey," she answers. "I really can get out of your hair. I was just burning up and needed a minute out of the sun."

Avery and I share a quick confused look because the girl in front of us has on a long-sleeved shirt and a pair of leggings. I thought maybe she was using them as a cover up in case the wind was a bit chilly early this morning, but it's over 95 degrees out here now so it's no wonder she's burning up.

"Uh, yeah, it's a hot one," I answer, "And we're Stella and Avery. Do you want a short-sleeved shirt or a cover up? Or I'm sure there's a swimsuit somewhere here on board if you need one."

Hailey looks like she's about to cry, but she just shakes her head. "No, no, it's fine. I just need a second to cool off and then I promise I'll go join the other girls and be out of your hair."

"Okay, that's no problem. Do you mind if we join you then?" Avery asks and Hailey shakes her head.

"Of course. I'm so sorry, I'm totally in the way," Hailey frets, and I notice the tears welling up in her eyes.

"Whoa, whoa, whoa. Hailey, it's okay. You're our guest, and if anything, we're the ones in the way. You sit here as long as you'd like, okay? Just take a deep breath," I encourage, and she gives me a weak smile.

"God, I'm such a disaster. I know I'm being so silly right now, but do you know when it just feels like everything is falling apart? I've just managed to get myself in this situation, and now, I'm looking back on the last few months and wondering how the hell I got here."

"Trust me, I think I might understand that more than you know," I say, and Avery smiles and wraps her arm around me.

"Yeah, you have no idea," Avery adds. "But do you want to talk about it? There's no pressure or anything—you just look really upset and sometimes all you need is a chat with someone completely outside of the situation to make you feel better."

"I don't want to bother you," Hailey protests.

"There's no pressure but you're definitely not bothering us. I know for me it helps to talk to someone completely removed from the situation when I'm really upset," I tell her.

"Oh, I hate to make the two of you sit around and listen to me complain about my shitty choices," Hailey sighs. "I just feel like I'm about to make the worst mistake of my life and I don't know how to stop it."

"Okay, that's it," Avery interjects, and I don't miss the concern on her face. My best friend may have a way of saying some really unhinged things, but she's also one of the most protective people I know, and I can tell she's not going to let this go without making sure the girl in front of us is okay. "I understand if you don't want to, but I'm actually asking you to try to explain what's going on."

Hailey hesitates across from us and finally, it's like a dam breaks and words start spilling too fast from her mouth.

"I got engaged two weeks ago, and I know if I marry him it's going to be a huge mistake. We met one night in a dive bar when I was in a really bad place, and for a while he was great. I'd just lost my job, and I didn't have any family or anything to call so I wasn't really sure how I was going to make ends meet. But then Ben and I hit it off, and he offered me a job at his business as a receptionist. After a few weeks of dating, he moved me into his apartment, and I really thought I was finally getting the life I've always dreamed of. But then things kinda took a turn."

My stomach tightens at that, and I try to brace myself for whatever she's about to tell us.

"Honestly, I'm probably being a little dramatic, but he's just become kinda controlling. And I know if I marry him, it'll just get worse. But it's not like I have many options. All of my friends are his friends. The girls on this trip are all wonderful, but Mia, the bride for this weekend, is Ben's cousin. So I feel like if I tried to talk through this to any of them, it just wouldn't go well."

Avery and I both sit quietly for a moment before Avery asks, "Okay, so when you say controlling, can you explain a little bit more about what you mean?"

I can tell my best friend is trying to stay calm, and I pat her leg under the table in silent encouragement and she knocks her knee against mine.

Hailey takes a deep breath before she answers. "Honestly, it sounds kinda silly, but here it is. It started with him telling me what to wear every day, which was fine because I was so grateful to have a job. And then he quit asking me what I wanted to eat or watch on television, which was such a small thing I didn't really notice for a few weeks. But then things kinda escalated from there."

I look at her long-sleeved shirt and the sweat pouring from her forehead before asking, "Does that have anything to do with why you're sweating your ass off right now?"

Hailey gives me a sad smile. "Yeah, Mia posted a picture of us at the pool yesterday on her Instagram and Ben saw it. He called me last night accusing me of whoring around on him and told me that if he saw another picture of me looking like a little slut we'd have problems when I got home. So I told the girls I was super sunburned and needed to wear something that covered me up, and did what he said. Don't get me wrong he doesn't hit me or anything, so I'm not really worried about that. But it just feels easier to go with what he wants at this point."

"Oh, hell no. Fuck that," Avery starts, and I kick her hard under the table to shut her up.

"Shit, Stels. That fucking hurt."

I give her a look, and she sighs, leaning back against the seat despite the fact that I know she's dying to keep going.

"What Avery means to say is, I completely understand why you would feel that way. But is that really what you want?" I ask, and Hailey sighs.

"Honestly, I don't know what I want. I love the friends I've made through him. I love having a job that I feel like I'm good at. I love knowing that, as long as I don't fuck it up, I could really have some stability after spending so long fending for myself. But I hate the way he makes me feel."

"I think that's all valid," I say with a small smile. "And it's honestly none of my business, but I think you deserve all of that and a man that doesn't make you feel like shit. You shouldn't have to choose between stability and happiness, Hailey."

"Damn right," Avery mutters under her breath, and Hailey lets out a small laugh.

"Yeah, I know you're right. But it's just so scary to put myself in a position to lose everything with him. Without even meaning to I kinda let him control my living situation, my job, my friends…everything. So even if I leave, I don't have anywhere to go."

"You can come here," Avery blurts before Hailey can continue. "We're looking to build a staff over the next few months and you could stay in the Hideaway until you're back on your feet. You don't have to marry some controlling asshole just to have your basic needs met."

I shoot Avery a look telling her to tone it down a little, and she just shrugs unapologetically. I don't mind that she made the offer, I'm just worried we're starting to overwhelm the girl sitting in front of us.

Hailey blinks at us both for a second before saying, "You

can't be serious. You've literally known me for less than twenty-four hours. Why in the hell would you offer all that?"

Avery opens her mouth to speak, but I hold up my hand and she leans back in her seat, obviously surrendering and letting me take over for a few minutes.

"I'm sorry, Avery can be a little blunt when she's upset. We're not trying to pressure you to make any major life changes. I know you barely know us, and we can't possibly understand how you're feeling. But if you decide you don't want to stay in your current situation, then our doors are always open to you, okay?"

Hailey smiles. "I really appreciate it. I don't think I'm ready to make a decision like that right now. But, honestly, I feel a little better after talking through it. I'm sorry I've kept you both so long, though. I know you have better things to do than sit around and listen to my bull shit."

"I totally get that, and stop. I'm glad you told us. So, now what do you say we try to have a little more fun on this trip, huh?"

CHAPTER 18
WYATT

"Cheers to a successful first weekend," I say the following night, holding up my beer and bumping it against Stella's lemonade.

"Hell yeah, we did," Avery interrupts before Stella can say anything, sliding into the booth beside her best friend, clinking her martini glass with ours.

"There they are. Scoot over, man. We're joining you," Bennett calls from by the bar and makes his way over with Trent following behind him.

"Damn it, when the hell did y'all get here?" I mutter under my breath as I scoot further into the booth. "I swear we can't go anywhere in this damn town without running into at least one of you."

"Come on, you know you love it," Bennett teases before adding, "Plus, there are exactly two restaurants in this town, and the last time we all went to Dune's Diner, they screwed up our order. So, The Sand Bar it is."

"Whatever," I mumble, not really caring they're here but feeling a little disappointed I won't have any alone time with

Stella until we get back to the cottage. We still haven't talked about the kiss last night, and all day, I felt like I was going to lose it if I didn't get to talk to her soon. So far we've both acted like nothing happened, but it's been less than twenty-four hours and I can already feel my control slipping when it comes to her.

All day I've thought about how good her sweet little body felt as she straddled my lap and kissed me like her life depended on it, but the longer the day's gone on, the more annoyed I've become that she's acting like it never happened. I know I sound like a fucking hypocrite because I also haven't acknowledged it yet, but damn it I just want to know what she's thinking. Does she regret it? If not, is it something she wants to happen again or was it a one-time thing? And has it consumed her every fucking thought today the way it has for me?

"Wyatt, hello? Did you hear me?" Bennett asks, waving his hand in front of my face to pull me from my thoughts.

"Huh?" I ask, and Bennett rolls his eyes at me.

"I knew you weren't listening. We're talking about going fishing one day this week when you don't have a charter. It's been ages since we went out there and the weather's supposed to be perfect."

"Yeah, I know I'm on the boat every day, but I haven't gone out for fun at all this year. I'm in," Trent adds. "I'm pretty sure tomorrow's our only day without anything though. Is that too last minute?"

"Nah, I can make that work," Bennett answers, turning back to me. "Wyatt, you in?"

"Uh, sure. That sounds good," I say, still partially distracted.

"Perfect, you boys can do that, and Stels and I will spend the day drinking seltzers by the ocean. I don't think we have any guests checking in tomorrow, and after the last few days, I need a day to relax."

"Same. I still can't believe we pulled it off," Stella says, smiling brightly. "That dinner on the beach almost did me in, but it ended up being really pretty."

"Yeah, lesson learned on checking the weather before we set up a four-course meal outside. But we made it work," Stella agrees and they both laugh.

"Wait, what happened?" Trent asks looking between both girls for an explanation.

"Well, we set up a long table with these beautiful place settings and strung lights down to the beach from the pool, but we didn't realize there was supposed to be a quick afternoon rain shower," Stella explains, wincing a little at the memory.

"How did the two of you move everything?" Bennett asks.

"We carried the table from the beach back to the pool and hid it under the cabana until the rain passed," Stella explains.

"Pretty sure I've never ran that fast in my damn life," Avery grumbles. "My calves are still sore from trying to run in the sand. I can't believe some people do that shit for fun."

"Wait, you mean it didn't inspire you to join me on my morning runs for the rest of the summer? I bet I could have you ready for a half marathon by Labor Day," Stella teases.

"Hell no," Avery answers, which causes Stella to giggle. "I'm perfectly content spending my mornings in bed like the rest of the world."

"Suit yourself," Stella teases. "So, what are—" she starts as she turns to me and the rest of the table before Avery interrupts her.

"Holy fucking shit," Avery yells, loud enough that the entire bar goes quiet and everyone turns to look at her.

It takes her a moment to realize how loud her outburst

was, and when she does she throws her hand up. "Oh, sorry," she yells before she turns back to us with her eyes wide.

"What the hell is going on?" I ask, concerned something is seriously wrong until Avery starts giggling uncontrollably.

"Aves, I'm gonna need you to fill us in ASAP," Stella adds, looking at her best friend with a mixture of concern and amusement.

"I just...went to ch-check the Instagram f—for the Hideaway," Avery chokes out between giggles. "Oh my god, there's no way this is real."

"Let me see," Stella insists, holding out her hand for Avery to give her the phone. She scrolls for a minute before she mutters under her breath. "Holy fucking shit."

Both girls giggle together for a second, and finally I snap. "For the love of God, could someone please fill the rest of us in?"

Stella takes a deep breath, her smile wider than I've seen it in a while. "I'm sorry, but I think we're both a little delirious from lack of sleep, and after our luck recently that post just doesn't seem real."

"What's the post about?" Trent asks.

Stella and Avery glance at each other, looking like they're about to start giggling again before Stella answers. "Apparently, one of the bridesmaids from this weekend is a major influencer. We're talking millions of followers. Well, she just posted a reel about the Hideaway a few hours ago and it's gone viral."

"What the hell does that mean?" I ask, looking between the girls. I've never been into social media so I'm not sure exactly what the big deal is.

"It means a shit ton of people watched the video," Trent answers.

"Well, I know that. But how many are we talking about? A

couple thousand?" I ask, looking between the girls and fighting the urge to roll my eyes as they start laughing again.

"Not quite. Actually, as of right now, it's at seven point two million views in less than six hours," Avery says, tapping at her phone screen. "And we've gained over nine thousand followers on the Hideaway's page too since she tagged us."

"Oh my god," Stella gasps. "This feels like a fever dream. Wait, did we get any reservations from it?"

Stella and Avery both freeze for a second, their eyes wide before Avery rushes to tap on her phone screen some more. After a moment her jaw drops and she sits there, frozen.

"Uh, Aves, I love you, but I'm pretty sure I've never seen you speechless. I'm going to need you to say something because I've gotta say, it's freaking me out a little," Stella says, looking nervously at her best friend.

After a moment, Avery looks up from her phone, her eyes wide. "Stels, we've had over thirty reservations made since lunch today. Plus, four bachelorette bookings. We're completely booked through the last weekend in July already starting next week."

I'm pretty sure no one at the table moves, as we all stare at each other in shock. After a moment, Stella blurts out, "There's no damn way this is real. You mean to tell me that, after just under a month of owning the hotel, some random bachelorette party happens to book the Hideaway? And one of those girls happens to be an influencer who posted a video about their stay at our hotel and it happens to go viral? And now we're booked?" she rambles, tears welling up in her eyes.

"Uh, yeah, I think that pretty much sums it up," Avery says. "And reservations are still rolling in, some of them all the way into next spring and summer."

After a moment, Stella looks at her best friend. "We're seriously booked?"

"Yep, babes, we are. From what I'm seeing there isn't a day left in the summer that we don't have any guests after this Wednesday," Avery answers, continuing to scroll through her phone. "And Wyatt and Trent, I have over forty messages asking for y'all's social media and website so they can book tours with you, not to mention the bridesmaid packages."

Now it's my turn to go quiet. Trent looks at me across the table, and I start to understand why Stella and Avery couldn't stop giggling. It's a weird feeling to think that one video could have such an impact on our lives, but here we are.

"Uh, I guess now's not a good time to tell you we don't have any of that shit?" I ask, wincing at the idea of losing all of those clients.

"Yeah, you do," Avery answers, her eyes wide. "I knew you'd fight me on it and tell me you didn't need any of that shit—which obviously, you do. So I just went ahead and drew up some branding and started a few social media pages for you last week. And I also found a way to tie your booking services into ours, so everyone who books with us has the option to also add on a charter. It's just not live yet, because I was planning to ask about it tonight."

I blink at her for a moment before asking, "Wait, you did all of that without talking to me?"

"Yep," Avery answers, popping the p. "And it took me hours, so you can just say thank you for all the business you're about to get. Or if you'd rather, I can reply to all of these people and tell them they'll have to call your number to set up a time. But I guarantee you won't get more than three phone calls."

"I swear to god, if your stubborn ass screws this up for

us," Trent mumbles under his breath, and that's enough to bring me back to my senses.

"No, you don't need to do that. I'm sorry. I was just caught off guard. But thank you, Avery. This really means a lot to us."

"No problem. Now I feel like we should do shots or something, right?" Avery asks, causing Stella and Bennett to laugh.

"Hell yeah, we do," Stella answers. "I need to run to the bathroom and I'll stop at the bar on the way back. Aves, can you let me out?"

Avery nods and Stella heads behind us in the direction of the bathroom.

"So, if it works for you, I can come by and show you how to work the software for future website bookings sometime next week. I can also make some tweaks to the logo while I'm there if there's anything in particular you want to see," Avery starts. We spend a few minutes going over what she's designed for us. The new logo is honestly a lot better than the one we currently have, and I'm impressed with the way she managed to tie in a fish hook and an illustration of the boat inside the words of Crestbrook Charter Company.

"That looks great, Avery," I say genuinely.

"Yeah, there's not a single thing I would do differently. Thank you again for taking this on for us," Trent agrees.

We talk for a few more minutes before I realize Stella still isn't back yet. Looking around the room, I see her standing over by the bar, waiting for our drinks.

"Damn, Everett must be short-handed tonight, it's taking her forever to grab those shots," Bennett says, following my gaze over to where she's standing. I don't love the slightly uncomfortable expression on her face, but due to other people standing around the bar, I can't see what's going on.

"Yeah, can you move and let me out? I'm going to check

on her," I announce, moving out of the booth and over to the bar. As I get closer, I start to have a pretty good idea of what had her looking upset. There's a man beside her I've never seen before, and he keeps leaning over to say something in her ear. Each time he does it, she scoots further away, but he follows her. I'm already holding back my anger at how uncomfortable she looks, but right as I step behind her, he grabs her arm and pulls her closer to him, looking at me warily.

"You've got about two seconds to get your hands off my wife before we have a serious fucking problem," I growl, and he looks up at me with wide eyes.

"Whoa, dude, we were just talking. No reason to be upset," the man says, clearly drunk and almost stumbling over himself as he holds up the hand not wrapped around Stella's arm in a sign of surrender.

"And while you were talking, did you not realize that she kept moving away from you? Or that she's wearing a fucking wedding ring?" I ask, my voice raising loud enough that most of the people around us freeze and turn to watch.

I'm vaguely aware that Everett is walking over from the other side of the bar, but all I can focus on is the fact that this asshole is still gripping Stella's arm. When she winces in pain at the way he squeezes her arm, I step forward, ready to do whatever I have to in order for him to leave Stella alone.

"Dude, what's got you so possessive of her? She's got a nice ass and all, but I'm sure I don't mind sharing if you don't —" the drunk guy starts, laughing to himself as Stella yanks her arm out of his hold and turns to kick him hard between the legs. He falls to the floor, and she stands over him, looking down on him like the trash that he is.

"First of all, I asked you nicely multiple times to leave me alone. And second of all, I wouldn't sleep with you if you were the last fucking man on earth. Maybe if you learned how to talk to a woman instead of addressing her like a piece of meat, you wouldn't be in this position right now," she says, and several of the people around the bar clap.

Everett leans down and grabs the man's shoulder. "Yeah, she said it better than I could, but you've gotta get the fuck out of here. And don't even think about coming back either."

As soon as the man's out of sight, Stella turns to me and gives me an apologetic look. "Sorry, I shouldn't have done that. I just didn't want you to feel like you needed to fight this battle for me too. But I'm so sorry I probably embarrassed you. And I'll apologize to Everett as well for doing that in his bar."

I blink at her in confusion. All the rage I was feeling just a minute ago has turned to possessive desire and I suddenly feel desperate to have her in my arms. I know I'm probably not thinking straight, but I don't give myself time to question what I know I'm about to do.

Leaning forward, I whisper in her ear, "Stella, that was the hottest fucking thing I've ever seen in my life. I was ready to handle it, but watching you stand up for yourself was fucking incredible. And I'm pretty sure if we don't get out of here right now, this whole damn bar is going to see how bad I want you."

CHAPTER 19
STELLA

Wyatt takes my hand and gently tugs me out of the bar while I hurry to keep up with him. Letting him lead, we make it to the truck and I lean against the cab while he opens my door. As soon as turns back to me, I pull him against me and feel his hard cock through his jeans.

"Damn it, Stella. We agreed we were going to ease into this, remember?" he groans. I look up at him through my lashes and shrug.

"I thought about it, and I don't want to wait if you don't," I mumble, teasing my hand up and down the front of his jeans.

He looks at me for a moment before whispering, "Fuck it." As soon as the words are out of his mouth, his mouth is on mine, and he lifts me so I can wrap my legs around his waist.

"Fuck, Stels. Do you have any idea how damn bad I've wanted you?" he asks, kissing down my neck, and I groan in contentment. "I'd give anything to rip this sweet little sundress off you and fuck you right here, but I won't ever forgive myself if the first time I feel that sweet pussy come around my cock is in a goddamned parking lot. So I need you to get in the car and let me drive you home so I can spend the rest of the night making you scream for me."

Damn, has this man always had a mouth like that? I wonder. "Sounds like a perfect night to me," I murmur, then pout when he sits me in the front seat of his truck and pulls back to walk around the front of the truck. As I watch him, I smile at the fact that my anxiety seems to be completely gone with him, and I feel my excitement build at the thought of finally having him inside me.

He cranks the truck and we ride in silence, neither of us wanting to break the spell between us. The ride to the Hideaway is less than five minutes, but tonight I'm pretty sure it takes an hour.

As soon as he pulls into the parking lot, I dive into his lap across the console and kiss him hard. I've never been this turned on in my life and I'm desperate to feel him everywhere.

"Come on, baby. Let's get you inside," he groans, easily lifting me off his lap to get out of the truck and he carries me across the dark parking lot. Every step he takes, I feel his hard cock pressing against me, and I resist the urge to moan as I imagine how good he's going to feel inside me.

He carries me across the property, and I press kisses against his neck as he fights to open the door of the cottage. "Fucking finally," he whispers, putting me down so he can push open the door and lead us inside. "I've never needed anyone more in my life."

"Same," I admit, reaching for his shirt and tugging it over his head. I let my hands wander down his bare chest, drifting lower until I palm his cock through his jeans. He sucks in a breath, and I smile at the sound.

"Are you being a tease?" he asks, and I lead him into the bedroom and close the door so that Duke won't interrupt us.

As soon as I turn around, Wyatt reaches down and tugs the hem of my dress over my head. "Damn it, Stels. Are you seriously not wearing any panties?"

I shake my head. "I didn't want panty lines."

"Jesus fucking Christ," he mumbles, running his hands up and down my sides. "You're so damn hot."

I lead him to the bed and sit on the edge to tug his jeans and boxers down. I try to stay in the moment, but as soon as he's naked my anxiety kicks in the same way it has every time I've had sex in the past.

Wyatt clearly notices the shift in my mood and sits down on the bed beside me, looking concerned.

"Hey, Stels. What the hell just happened?" he asks, and I try to avoid eye contact, completely embarrassed with the way I'm shutting down. "If you don't want to do this, we absolutely don't have to."

"No, it's not that," I admit, sighing before I continue. "My anxiety just gets really high when it comes to sex sometimes. I get really nervous about how long it takes me to get there and then I worry I'm not doing something right. Then my brain starts going, and I can't focus on anything and I basically spiral from there. And now, here I am freaking out like an idiot when all you want is to fuck me."

"Whoa, Stels. It's okay. Just take a breath, okay?" he says, rubbing my back.

"God, you have to think I'm the biggest mess in the world," I say, trying to resist the urge to cry. "I'm sorry. I really want to do this, but I'm worried I'm going to mess it up."

"Hey, there's nothing to mess up here, Stels. Everything's

at your pace. Do I want you? Hell fucking yes. And if all you want to do tonight is go to bed, that's fine."

"No, I want to do this. But it can take me a really long time to get there," I warn, my cheeks flaming with embarrassment at the words.

"Stels, I don't care about that," he tells me. "Do you trust me?"

"Yeah, of course," I tell him, feeling a little of the anxiety that was building inside me start to fade.

"Okay, we're gonna try something. Just lie back and close your eyes," he instructs, and I do as he says.

It feels weird to lie here, not knowing what he's doing, and I resist the urge to peek as I hear him dig through a drawer somewhere in the room.

I freeze when I hear the familiar buzz of my vibrator and jump as he presses it to my clit.

"Holy shit, Wyatt," I cry and open my eyes to see him kneeling above me.

"Just relax, okay, Stels?" he tells me, and I try to do as he asked.

The toy buzzes insistently against my clit, and I start to get lost to the feeling before he reaches up and starts to work his fingers inside of me, matching the pulses of the vibrator with the thrusts of his fingers.

"God, you're fucking soaked," he murmurs. "You have such a pretty pussy, Stella."

I moan and feel myself relaxing more and more the longer he touches me. I lose track of time as he fucks me with his fingers and tells me I'm a good girl over and over. After a while, I feel my core tighten, and my eyes pop open in surprise.

"Oh my god, Wyatt, I think I'm going to come," I moan,

and he smiles, continuing to work his fingers in and out of me as the vibrator pulses against my clit.

"That's right, pretty girl. Come for me. I want to feel you soak my fingers," he whispers, and with that, the climax takes over my body and I'm lost to the feeling of ecstasy that takes over my body.

I'm vaguely aware of the fact that I'm moaning loud enough that the guests in the hotel nearby can probably hear, but I'm too fucking gone to care. I've never come this hard in my damn life.

By the time I come back to my senses, I don't know if the moment between us lasted minutes or hours, but I can't find it in myself to care.

"That was fucking incredible, Stels. You're so pretty when you come," Wyatt mutters, dropping a kiss to my forehead. I blush a little at the words, reaching to touch him.

"You don't have to," Wyatt mutters. I ignore him, shifting to my knees on the bed and leaning down to wrap my mouth around his shaft.

"Fuck, Stels," he moans, and I use that as encouragement to take him deeper. I use my hand to tease the base of his cock and he places his hand on the back of my head, but doesn't put any pressure on me to take him deeper.

Bobbing up and down on his cock, I lick and taste and suck at him, desperate to feel him lose himself after how good he made me feel.

"Shit, I'm about to come," he warns, but I continue tasting him, looking up at him through my lashes to let him know I don't want to stop.

"Fuck," he curses, as hot cum starts to fill my mouth. He growls as he comes, and I continue sucking him until he pulls away, obviously finished.

"Holy shit, Stels. You're so fucking incredible," he

murmurs, dropping a kiss to my mouth. "Let's get cleaned up and then we're doing that again."

"OH MY GOD, I'm pretty sure this is what dreams and orgasms are made of," Avery says, collapsing into her beach chair the following day.

"That's quite a combination, Aves," I say, unable to help myself from laughing at her.

"Yeah, yeah. Speaking of orgasms, I'm going to need all the details on what happened after Wyatt carried you out of the bar like a damn caveman. If I wasn't ready to give you a standing ovation for the way you handled that asshole, I'd be totally pissed you abandoned me."

"I really am sorry about that," I apologize, sitting down in my chair and reaching for a cooler Wyatt packed for us earlier this morning. I'm about to grab a seltzer when I see the familiar orange and blue can of my favorite energy drink.

Pausing, I pull it out and Avery looks over to give me an odd look. "I thought you couldn't find them anywhere."

"I couldn't," I respond. "Wyatt offered to pack the cooler this morning, but there's no way he found them for me. Maybe there was one in the fridge I missed yesterday."

"Well, obviously it didn't appear out of thin air, Stels. Text him and see what he says."

Pulling out my phone, I shoot him a quick text.

Stella: Hey, I just looked in the cooler. Did I miss one of my drinks in the fridge on Saturday? I would have sworn that there weren't any left but maybe I was wrong.

Wyatt: Oh no, you didn't.

I look at Avery in confusion, showing her the text.

"Damn girl, see. I told you he's down bad for you. Where the hell did he find them though?" Avery asks, grabbing a black cherry seltzer out of the cooler and popping the top.

"I have no idea."

"Well, babes, why don't you ask him?" my best friend suggests.

"Oh, right. Yeah, that would make sense."

Stella: Uh, is there some secret energy drink supply store here in town that I don't know about? Because I would have sworn up and down that I checked everywhere in town the other day.

Wyatt: Nope, not quite.

Stella: ….

Stella: Wyatt, how the hell did you find them?

Wyatt: It's not a big deal. I called Everett on Saturday when we got back from the boat tour, and he called in a favor with one of his distributors. They added a couple cases to his order this morning so you should be good to go for a while.

Stella: Oh my gosh.

Stella: Are you serious?

Stella: I want to kiss you right now.

Stella: Thank you so much Wyatt. And tell Everett thank you and to let me know how much I owe him.

Wyatt: Don't worry about it, I already took care of it.

Wyatt: But I will take that kiss when you get home tonight.

"Damn, Stels. What spell did you manage to put on the poor boy?" Avery teases, leaning over to read the messages over my shoulder.

I roll my eyes at her before I text him back.

Stella: Deal ;)

I throw my phone back in my bag and grab the drink out of the cooler, taking a long sip and smiling.

"Did you hear back from Chloe?" Avery asks. "I know you said you were going to invite her this morning, but I didn't know if she replied."

"Yeah, she said she had to check in with some of the lifeguards this morning but she should be here soon. I'm glad she's coming."

"Me too. We could use some other girlfriends, especially if you're planning to start abandoning me to roll around in the sheets with that hubby of yours," Avery teases, and I roll my eyes at her.

"That's not exactly what happened," I say hesitantly.

"Babes, I love you, but don't even act like you didn't get some last night."

I blush and finally decide to say screw it.

"Fine, we might have a moment or two, but we agreed it's just for fun. Friendly, casual, meaningless, sex."

"Pshh, yeah, I'm sure that's gonna go super well, Stels," Avery says sarcastically. "The two of you are married and he's getting his brother to track down his supplier to buy you those damn drinks. And you're still gonna be living together for the next eleven months? Sounds totally casual and meaningless to me."

"Hey, y'all," Chloe calls, coming up behind us and dropping her small beach bag in the sand. "Sorry, I'm late. One of my lifeguards was twenty minutes late for his shift, so I had to wait until he got there. But anyway, what'd I miss?"

"We were just talking about Stels having hot sex with her fake husband. She thinks it doesn't mean anything, but we both know that man is obsessed with her," Avery interjects before I can say anything and I shoot her a look of frustration.

"Damn, Aves, we want Chloe to be our friend, not run her off the first time she hangs out with us," I say, rubbing my face with my hand.

Avery shrugs. "Sorry, I figured it'd be best to just throw her straight in. We both know there's no point in pretending I have a filter."

Chloe looks between us for a moment, and I'm afraid she's going to leave as quickly as she came, but instead, she bursts into laughter.

"Oh my god, this is exactly what I've been missing. I'm so damn glad you two moved here. But wait, I need us to back up. What do you mean fake husband? I thought y'all got married?" she asks, and I sigh.

"It's kind of a long story. Wyatt and I weren't in the mood to give the whole run down to the town, so I'll totally tell you, but can you promise to keep it between us?"

"Of course. I'll be honest, outside of the teenagers who lifeguard for me, I don't have much social interaction. Whatever you say is totally safe with me," she promises.

I give her a quick rundown of the last month, and she looks at me with wide eyes as I talk about the hotel and the fake wedding, and all the way up to the events at the bar last night.

"Oh my god. This is wild! Nothing like this ever happens in Crestbrook!" Chloe says, and I laugh.

"Yeah, it's definitely all a little out of the ordinary. But last night we agreed to meaningless sex for the rest of the time while we're married," I admit, and Chloe laughs.

"Oh yeah, sorry Stella, but you two are totally fucked. I know you've been gone a while, but over the last few years, Wyatt's become totally withdrawn from everything in town, and just kinda a grump. I know he puts all of this pressure on himself to take care of his brothers. And I'll be honest, you saw how much everyone in this town has been struggling to make ends meet recently. But everyone in this town has noticed how different he is around you."

"See, I told you, Stels," Avery says matter-of-factly.

"I think you're both overreacting. Sure, we've always gotten along, but I don't think he feels that way about me," I insist.

Avery and Chloe look at each other before Avery rolls her eyes. "Yeah, I'm sure that's all it is. But even if that's true, you still haven't told us how you feel about him."

I hesitate, knowing if I admit the truth to Avery, she'll never let it go. "Yeah, I guess I like him a little."

"Stella Elizabeth Hale Robinson," Avery yells and I laugh at her use of my full name with the addition of Wyatt's last name.

"Uh, Aves, you know I didn't actually change my name, right?" I ask, and she shrugs.

"Yeah, whatever. Enough of that. Come on and be honest. You know we don't keep secrets in this friendship."

Sighing, I decide to give in. "Fine, there are definitely some feelings there, but I'm not ready to dissect them yet. I'm still getting adjusted to living in Crestbrook Cove and we're about to be so busy with the hotel that I just want to enjoy how things are for a while before I put any more pressure on everything," I admit, and Chloe nods encouragingly.

"I think that's a good point, Stella. You and Avery have both been through a lot of changes over the last month, and I don't think there's anything wrong with not wanting to rush anything," she says, and I smile at her in gratitude.

"Fine, I'll allow it," Avery says, obviously content with the information she was able to get out of me already. "So, now that that's taken care of, we need to talk about the Hideaway for a minute."

"Wait, is something wrong?" Chloe asks, looking between us in concern.

"Actually, for once, I don't think so," I say with a laugh. "We just hosted our first bachelorette trip and apparently one of the girls is some major influencer, and she made a post about the Hideaway. Well, it went viral and now we need to figure out how we're going to staff all the bookings we got from it."

"Wait, so you actually need a full staff? How many reservations are we talking?" Chloe asks.

Avery pulls out her phone. "I actually haven't let myself check any of the numbers because I wanted to be with Stels when I did. But last night before I went to bed, there were over seventy-five reservations made yesterday."

Chloe's mouth drops open in surprise. "Are you serious?

This hotel hasn't had more than ten rooms booked out at a time since I was in high school."

"Yeah, it's not what we expected, but we're still grat—" I start before Avery interrupts me with a loud scream.

"Damn it, Aves. You've gotta quit doing that," I complain, looking over and waiting for her to fill us in.

"Stels," she says, looking up at me, "we're almost completely booked from the Fourth of July next weekend until the end of August. We've also already got bookings for spring break and next summer. Plus, ten bachelorette requests and I've gotten four wedding inquiries for next summer too."

I stare at her in shock. "No, that can't be right."

"Yeah, it actually is," she argues, her smile spreading.

"Wait, how many reservations came in since last night?" I ask, trying to make sense of what she's saying.

Avery taps at her phone for a moment before answering, "Another sixty-five and counting. And we're up to almost twenty thousand followers on Instagram."

With that, I can't control the laughter that bubbles out of me. "This can't be fucking real," I wheeze out through the mixture of laughter and tears I feel building. "Aves, how the hell are we going to make this happen with exactly two-and-a-half staff members?"

"Wait, we're gonna come back to how fucking incredible this is, but I've gotta know, who's the half?" Chloe asks, looking between us.

"Kelly, the housekeeper has just been coming in on an as needed basis," I explain, then add, "oh my gosh, I'm actually gonna have to call Miss Clara and ask her for help."

"Well, that may be a possibility," Avery mutters. "All I know is we have a few guests coming in this week, and after that, the next six weeks are nonstop. So we'd better find some staff before that."

"What are we going to do, Aves?" I ask, trying not to panic.

"Wait, wait, wait. I know this is a little overwhelming, but do the two of you not understand how fucking incredible this is?" Chloe asks, looking between us. "Or how many other businesses this could help? Not just Wyatt's business, but they have to eat somewhere. And Bennett's surf shop? We could even get some new businesses if we actually have enough tourism to support them."

Avery and I pause, neither of us realizing how far-reaching this could be for Crestbrook Cove.

"Yeah, I didn't really think about it like that, but you're right," I admit.

"I know I am," Chloe teases before opening her bag. "Listen, I stopped by The Sand Bar and had Everett make us a gallon of that yummy pineapple vodka lemonade he makes. I say we spend the next hour drinking and tanning, and then tomorrow you drop the news to Miss Agatha that you need help. Have her put it in the *The Cove Column*. I guarantee you won't have any problem finding people to help you. Personally, I know I'll even help out where I can."

"I'm gonna have to take your word on that one," Avery says hesitantly.

I smile, knowing Chloe's right. "Actually, I agree with her. With the way this town gossips, once we get the word out, I think we'll have the help we need. Now, let's spend a little while drinking away our problems and get ready to work our asses off."

CHAPTER 20
WYATT

"Okay, Miss Clara, can you take these towels to Room 204? And Miss Agatha, Room 210 asked for us to deliver them some extra toiletries if you don't mind," Stella says from behind the front desk of the Hideaway, giving out orders.

It's been just over a month since the video of the Hideaway went viral, and I still can't believe how quickly everything changed around here. As soon as word got out that we needed help, Miss Clara came through with a list of ladies from her knitting club who were willing to volunteer a few days a week to make sure we could take care of all the guests. It's not the most conventional, but the ladies seem to enjoy interacting with everyone and Stella claims it's added an extra layer of local flair to the stay.

As I look at my wife, I try to ignore the feeling of unease I feel with how fast this year is flying by. We've already been married for over two months, and each day I worry a little more about how I'm going to walk away at the end of the year like I promised. We spend all our time together outside of work, eating dinner with our friends at The Sand Bar and walking Duke at night around the hotel before we head to bed where we spend hours fucking and whispering into the night.

Neither of us has acknowledged the shift in the relationship, but I know I can't keep pretending that there's nothing between us anymore. There's nothing friendly about the way I feel about Stella, and the idea of losing her next year makes me feel a lot more lost than I'd like to admit.

The older ladies smile at Stella before heading over to the elevators, and I take advantage of the lull in customers to head over to Stella and wrap her from behind with a hug. "Hey there, what are you doing here?" she asks with a laugh. "I thought you had a tour this afternoon."

"I do. Trent had a booking earlier this afternoon and he needed me to drive the van," I say, making a face. When all the hotel guests started booking booze cruises, we realized we needed a safe way to transport people between the docks and the Hideaway thanks to the lack of Uber in Crestbrook. Trent found an old fifteen-passenger van to run back and forth for cheap on Marketplace and it's worked out pretty well for us. But since he knows I despise driving the damn thing, he usually takes care of it.

Stella laughs at my expression, and I take advantage of the empty lobby and pull her into the small office behind the counter to kiss her hard.

"Wyatt, I can't leave the counter for more than a second. We have a party that should be getting here any minute," she objects at the same time she leans against the wall and wraps her leg around my waist to pull me closer to her.

"Just for a second," I promise, devouring her mouth and running my fingers through her hair to hold her to me.

She moans slightly as our tongues tangle in the dark office

space before she finally pulls back. "Okay, we've gotta stop. We need to be professionals here, Wyatt."

Instead of pulling away, she drops one more kiss on my mouth and leans in to hug me close for another moment before slipping out the door.

"Come on, hubby," she teases, waiting for me to follow her out of the office. "We need to get back to work, but we can finish this after the party on the beach for Avery's birthday tonight."

I groan at the reminder. "Damn it, is that tonight? I was looking forward to coming straight home and spending the night with those pretty legs wrapped around me."

"Yes, well, as fun as that sounds…" she says, "you and I both know there's no way we're missing Avery's party. And even if we tried, she would one million percent hunt us down and drag us out of the cottage, dressed and ready or not."

I shudder. "Actually, now that I think about it, you're right. I know she's your best friend and all, but she still scares me."

Stella laughs loudly just as the front door opens and over twenty guests pile in, heading toward the check-in counter. "Oh, she knows," she teases. "I'll see you at the cottage tonight."

"Hey, Stels, are you almost ready to go?" I call through the house. I just got back from taking Duke for a walk, and I'm anxious to get this party over with so I can have Stella to myself.

"Almost," she yells, and Duke takes off to search for her. I follow him into the bathroom, and my breath catches when I see how fucking gorgeous she looks.

Her pink swimsuit accentuates every inch of her toned body, and the white open-front skirt she's wearing with it makes her look fucking incredible.

"Damn, Stels," I mutter, and she turns to smile at me.

"Oh, hi. Sorry, I'm almost ready. Does this look okay?" she asks, spinning to let me see her from several different angles.

"Stella, you look fucking incredible. Are you sure we have to go to this party? I'd much rather keep you here."

She laughs and rolls her eyes. "Yeah, that would go so well for me. You know Avery would freak if we didn't show up. Plus, she told me it's supposed to be a super small event. I think she just invited your brothers, Bennett, and Chloe."

"Oh, that's it?" I ask, slightly surprised. "She did all this work just for the seven of us?"

"Yeah…you've met Avery, right? Does it seem like she does anything halfway to you?" Stella points out, and I shrug in agreement.

"Okay, fine, you may have a point," I admit.

"Yeah, I know I do," she teases. "But anyway, I'm ready now. You ready to walk?"

Duke's head pokes up just as I say his favorite "w" word and his tail starts beating against the floor in excitement.

"Buddy, you can't go with us to the party, but I promise we won't be gone too long and then we'll play," Stella says to her dog, leaning over to pet him.

"I know, I'm sorry," she says before straightening and looking at me. "All right, let's get going."

We walk back into the bedroom and I freeze when I see the new addition.

"Stella, what the fuck is that on the wall?" I ask, my eyes wide.

"Oh, I almost forgot. Look at what I finally got back from the frame shop," she says, gesturing to the wall where the caricature of the two of us from the wedding sign that was attached to the boat the day after our wedding now hangs proudly over the bed. She had them trim it down to just the drawing, and I'll admit she looks pretty cute in the picture. But me on the other hand? I have buck teeth and a nose that takes up half the page.

"Is this really necessary, Stels?" I ask, already knowing this is probably not an argument I'm going to win.

"Of course it is. Look how cute we are," she says, looking up at it with a wide smile.

"How in the hell did you even find the damn thing?" I ask, and Stella laughs.

"Trent thought it was too good to pass up, so he saved it when he took it down and brought it to me," Stella explains. All I can do is shake my head.

"Fucking traitor," I mutter. "Anyway, can we go now?"

"Sure," Stella agrees. "Just lead the way."

We make the quick walk down to the beach, and my jaw drops when I see the crowd of people standing around and grabbing drinks across the beach.

"Okay, that's definitely more than ten people," I point out, and Stella stares ahead of me in shock.

"Yeah, it definitely is," Stella agrees. "Do you think Miss Agatha put something in the paper again?"

"If someone told her about it, I think it's a pretty good possibility," I say in response, and Stella's eyes widen.

"God, this town is really something. Let's go find Aves," she suggests. I follow her through the party, looking for her best friend. Finally, after what feels like forever, Stella spots her and runs over.

"Happy birthday, Aves," Stella says, wrapping Avery in a hug and kissing her on the cheek. "This is some party, huh?"

"I'll say. Where the hell did all of these people come from?" I ask, looking around at the still growing crowd.

"Well, Miss Clara heard me talking about it at work today, and I told her that she could come by if she wanted to. But apparently, tonight is the same night as her knitting club, so she told all the ladies to come, and then it grew from there. Honestly, they all brought their own alcohol, so I don't really mind the extra guests."

Stella laughs and looks through the crowd. "Aves, it looks like the nursing home edition of *Sports Illustrated* in here. I've never seen this many elderly ladies in a bikini."

"Same." Avery laughs. "Honestly, I think it's fucking fabulous. I stand by the fact that I hope I have that kind of confidence when I'm their age."

"Wait," I interject. "If Miss Clara invited all of her friends, does that mean Miss Eleanor is here?"

I look around panicked while Avery gives me a funny look. "I can't keep up with all the older ladies in town, Wyatt. I'm sorry, but which one is she?"

"The one who objected at our wedding because she has a ginormous crush on my husband," Stella says and she and Avery both break into a fit of giggles at that.

"Oh my god. I almost forgot about that. But yeah, I'm sure she's here somewhere," Avery answers.

"Fuck," I curse just as Miss Clara and Miss Eleanor make their way over to us.

"Happy birthday, Avery," Miss Clara says with a wide smile while Miss Eleanor just glares at Stella.

"Thank you, Miss Clara," Avery says, trying not to laugh at the current encounter.

"Wyatt, are you planning to save a dance for me tonight?" Miss Eleanor asks, and I feel my eyes widen at her question.

"As fun as that sounds, I don't think I'll have time," I tell her. trying desperately to get her to leave me alone.

"We'll see about that," she mutters under her breath, before turning to Avery. "Happy birthday, dear. Thank you so much for having us."

"Of course, y'all enjoy," Avery says, smiling widely at them as they meander further into the party. As soon as they're gone, she turns to me with wide eyes.

"Oh my god, that was fucking hilarious. She's like actually into you," she says. Stella covers her mouth to keep her giggle from spilling out.

"I need a fucking drink," I mutter, and both girls finally dissolve into laughter.

"I love this place a little more every day," Stella admits. "Now, let's grab a drink before Miss Eleanor comes by and scoops you up."

"COME ON, we've gotta get out of here," I whisper to Stella a few hours later. I've spent more time avoiding Miss Eleanor over the last few hours than I've spent with Stella, and I'm more than ready to strip Stella down, and spend the next few hours giving her body the attention it deserves.

"Okay, yeah, let's go. It's been kind of a long day and Avery looks like she's having a great time," she says, gesturing to where her best friend is dancing on top of the makeshift stage, singing and dancing with a few of the locals

I haven't met yet. "Let me just text her that we're leaving and we'll go."

"Perfect," I tell her before lowering my voice. "I've spent all night looking at how fucking sexy you are and I'm gonna lose it if I don't get my hands on you."

Stella blushes and grabs my hand, leading me back through the woods to the cottage. Every few steps, she stops and pulls me down to kiss me hard before continuing on her way.

"Shit, Stels, I want you so damn bad," I mutter, trying to hold her to me but since she's still in her swimsuit, the slick fabric helps her slip out of my grip.

"Come on, Wyatt. If we start out here, I won't want to stop and some of the guests could see us," she argues. I grab her hand to let her lead us, knowing she's right.

I follow her back to the cottage, where she guides me to the small alcove where there's an outdoor shower we use to rinse the sand off from the beach. As soon as we step behind the wooden partition that shields us from the rest of the path, I pull her to me and kiss her hard.

"Fucking finally," I murmur. "All I've thought about since we left the house is getting you out of this swimsuit, Stels."

She smiles, turns on the water, and drags me under the cool stream of the shower. After spending the last few hours in the late evening heat, I groan at the feeling of the cool water against my overheated skin and Stella shivers in my arms.

"Cold?" I ask, and she shakes her head, dropping her hands down to tug on my swim trunks. As soon as I'm free of them, she runs her fingers across my already hard shaft, and I suck in a breath at the contact.

Unable to wait any longer, I tug her swimsuit top off and pop her pink nipple into my mouth. She threads her fingers through my hair, and I smile as I feel her give herself over to me. It turns out that once Stella's comfortable, her anxiety doesn't seem to be an issue anymore—at least when it comes to sex. There've been times where she freezes, and we've worked through them, but for the most part, she seems to become more excited and carefree each time we're together.

"Please fuck me, Wyatt," Stella mutters after I've teased her for a few moments, and that's all the encouragement I need to pull her swimsuit down and slide inside her.

When Stella and I started having sex, she insisted that I didn't need to wear a condom thanks to her birth control, and every time I feel her hot pussy wrap around my cock, I'm convinced I'll never feel anything this fucking incredible again in my life.

"Shit, Wyatt," she moans as soon as I'm inside her. "You feel so fucking good."

I murmur my agreement, leaning down to grab her legs and wrap them around my waist, pressing her back against the wooden wall of the shower. The water beats down around us, and the combination of the sensations of the water and her body have me ready to come already.

"You look so pretty when you take my cock, Stels," I whisper in her ear and grunt when I feel her pussy spasm around my cock. "God, you're so fucking tight. Were you thinking about this while we were down at the beach? Because you're all I've thought about all fucking night."

"Yes, I wanted you too," she moans between thrusts, and I can tell she's close. Reaching down, I play with her clit, and I feel her spasm with the first wave of her orgasm.

"Shit, Wyatt, don't stop," she begs. I use her words as encouragement to hold off until she's finished. As soon as I feel her orgasm start to wane, I let out a sigh of relief and start to fuck her harder, losing myself to my own orgasm. I feel my cum spill into her tight pussy and I lean against the wall to support us both as we come down from the high of our orgasms.

"You did so good, Stels," I tell her, pressing a kiss to her forehead and she smiles at my praise.

"I don't think that'll ever get old," Stella says with a laugh. I try to hide my wince at the reminder that she's right. It already feels like time's running out on this arrangement, and I'm afraid I won't ever get enough of her.

CHAPTER 21
STELLA

"God, this is exactly what I needed," I groan, sinking into the booth at The Sand Bar later that week. "A pineapple vodka lemonade and some greasy french fries are calling my name."

"Ugh, same," Avery agrees. "I can't remember the last time we sat down and had drinks together. The last month has been such a damn whirlwind."

"Right? Can you believe we've been running the Hideaway together for over two months? Sometimes I still feel like we're in our first week here, and other times it feels like we've been here for years."

"Yeah, same. I was thinking about that earlier this week. It's hard to believe that if we hadn't lost our jobs at the beginning of the summer, we would be getting ready to go back to school at Smith's Valley," Avery points out.

"God, isn't that wild? I've just gotta say, I know the last month has been a little chaotic, but I already can't imagine this not being our lives. Is that weird? I mean, don't get me wrong, I will probably totally be in my feels on the first day of school and I'll probably always miss the kids, but I wasn't expecting to feel this much peace with not going back to the classroom.

Avery nods in agreement. "Yeah, I totally feel that. I really did love teaching, but I feel so much less stressed already knowing I don't have to go back. And now that our bookings are up so much, we actually aren't as broke as I thought we'd be."

I can't help but laugh at that. "I still can't believe you moved down here with me with literally no guarantee of a salary or benefits or anything, Aves. I really don't know how I'll ever thank you. There's no way on earth I could have done this by myself."

"Aww, Stels, you know there was no way I was letting you do this alone. I'm actually having a great time coming up with new ideas for the Hideaway, and even with how busy we've been, I've started working on building up my art business too. It's really been a win for both of us. Plus, if I hadn't moved, I would've missed the entertainment of watching you pretend that you aren't totally in love with your not-so-fake husband."

I roll my eyes. "Lord, here we go again. Are you ever going to just believe me when I say we're happy with how things are now? We don't have to be anything more."

I know as I say the words that they aren't completely true, but they've become such a habit, that they fall easily from my lips.

The truth? I've been falling for Wyatt over the last few months. He's sweet and funny, and he makes me feel so special when we're together. Not to mention the fact that the sex is fucking incredible. No one's ever made me feel the way he has, but I try to remind myself that after the end of the year, all of this goes away. No more spending Sunday mornings in bed seeing how many times he can make me come. No more afternoon walks with Duke around the property, laughing about the different shenanigans from the day around the hotel.

Avery looks across the table at me, taking a sip of her lemonade before she asks, "Stels, I love you, but can we drop the act? You're in love with your husband, and the sooner you acknowledge it, the sooner we can figure out what we're going to do about it."

"I—I'm def—definitely not in love with him," I sputter, completely taken aback by her accusation. "Sure, I have a little bit of a crush, but have you seen the man? He's fucking gorgeous. And he's done so much for me and the hotel, and the sex is great, but that's it. We promised we were just friends, Aves. You know that," I continue to ramble as Avery watches me skeptically.

"Babes, let's be real. You're in love with him. And there's nothing wrong with that. But I do think we need to move past the denial phase we're currently in because delusion isn't cute on ya," she says.

I blink at her and realize she's right. I've known I was developing feelings, but when she lays it out in front of me, I can't deny it to myself any longer. I'm completely in love with Wyatt Robinson, and I don't know if my heart's going to survive losing him. But at the same time, there's no way I can ask him to stay with me. He's already given up a year of his life to make sure I get to keep the Hideaway, and we've both been super clear with the expectation that all of this ends in just ten months.

Desperate to ignore the panic rising in my chest at the thought, I shoot her an ugly look. "Did you bring me here just to stage an intervention?"

"Not quite. I really did want a night out with you. Other

than my party earlier this week, I feel like I haven't seen you outside of work since the hotel took off. But, I also can't ignore how worried I am about you. I don't want you to get hurt, Stels."

I grab her hand from across the table. "I know, Aves, and I really appreciate it. But it'll be okay. And if it's not, I know I can count on you to bring the ice cream and the wine, right?"

"Damn right, you can. You know you're never getting rid of me."

I smile and look down at my lap to see my phone ringing. "Oh, hold on. My Uncle Allen's calling me."

Avery looks back at me in confusion. "The one from Springside? I didn't think the two of you chatted all that often."

"We don't. Let me see what he wants and make sure nothing's wrong," I tell her, answering the phone.

"Hello?"

"Hey, Stella. I know it's late so I won't keep you long," he starts, and I look down at the time to see it's barely seven in the evening.

"It's fine. What's going on? Is everything okay?" I ask, wondering if he's calling to tell me something happened to my dad. Since I don't have any contact with him, Uncle Allen is about the only one who would think to call me.

"Oh no, nothing like that. I'm actually calling because I know you were looking for a teaching position earlier this summer. Two of my teachers here in Springside just resigned and teacher work days start next week. I know it's last minute and you're living in Crestbrook Cove now, but I felt like I need to at least give you the option in case you and your friend still want something in the classroom. And I'm not gonna lie, I'm really in a bind and you'd kinda be helping me out here."

I blink in surprise, not sure what to say. Earlier in the summer, I would have really had to think about it. But after the last few months of working with the hotel and feeling my anxiety lessen as I spend more time away from the school, there's not a doubt in my mind I'm doing what I'm supposed to be doing here in Crestbrook Cove.

"Uncle Allen, I really appreciate it, but I feel like I've found my home in Crestbrook. Plus, if I walk away from the Hideaway, Memaw's will said that I forfeit the hotel. So I'm sorry, but I can't do that right now. But if you're looking for someone, I can send you a few names of people who might be interested."

"Oh, I didn't realize. My momma did really have a sense of humor, didn't she? But no worries. I'd appreciate those names, though, if you have time," he says.

"Sure thing. Talk to you later," I say before hanging up and turning to Avery.

"So, in case you're wondering if the universe has a sense of humor, we just got teaching offers in Springside. I guess I should've checked with you before I turned it down," I chuckle. "These last few months have really thrown us some curveballs, huh?"

"Girl, I just told you, there's no way I'm leaving you. Plus, the idea of going back to turning in lesson plans and sitting through lunch duty again gives me hives. I promise I'm good."

"Honestly, same. It's so weird how that was everything I thought I wanted just two months ago. Maybe one day, I'll decide to go back into the classroom. But for right now, I'm happy with our life."

"Me too," Avery agrees. "You know, I'm pretty sure this is the first thing we've said no to all summer."

I laugh, realizing she's right. "Oh gosh, I haven't even

thought about that. But you know, I think with everything we've accomplished the last few months, we definitely made the best of our summer."

"Hell yeah we did," Avery says, holding up her drink, "Cheers to new adventures."

CHAPTER 22
WYATT

"Hey, do you need anything else tonight?" Trent asks as we finish rinsing off the boats. "I need to run to the parts house before they close for some extra fuel filters."

"Nope, I'm good. But would you also pick up some spark plugs just in case? The *Fin and Tonic* seems to be doing much better than she was earlier this summer, but I don't want to get stranded with all the new tours we've been taking on," I explain, turning off the water hose.

"Sure, no problem. I'll bring them in with me on Monday. Are we still on for brunch at the pier tomorrow?"

"Damn it. My wife and her best friend really have the ability to plan some shit don't they," I groan, remembering Stella and Avery planned a day with our friends tomorrow since we all finally have a day off. I'd been looking forward to having her to myself, but there was a new breakfast restaurant down by the water that our guests have been raving about, and I forgot I promised Stella we could all go together.

My brother chuckles then says, "You know, I've gotta

admit, it's pretty fun seeing the way you're completely wrapped around her finger. I never thought I'd see the day where you let yourself be happy, but I'm sure as hell glad you did, man."

"Yeah, yeah, whatever you say," I reply, feeling slightly uncomfortable with the serious turn this conversation took.

"Don't get me wrong you're still a grumpy ol' asshole at times," Trent teases, and I laugh, flipping him off. "In all seriousness, I do think you two are good together. But what's going to happen at the end of this year? Are you really going to let her go?"

"Well, that's what we agreed on," I say, trying not to think about how much I'm dreading everything with Stella coming to an end.

"Just think about it, man. I just don't want you to get hurt if this doesn't go the way you've planned."

"Thanks. I'll be okay," I mutter, not sure if I'm trying to convince him or myself.

"Whatever you say. Either way, I guess we'll figure it out. I've gotta run. I'll see you tomorrow," my brother says before hopping off his boat and heading down the pier, leaving me to finish cleaning the boats by myself.

I grab an extra cloth out of the glove box and start to wipe down the seats before I head in for the day. Usually, this part of my day is spent going through my to-do list for the next day's charters, but today I can't seem to stop thinking about Stella. My wife has consumed more and more of my thoughts over the last few weeks and I'm starting to feel like a man obsessed.

I try not to let myself think too hard about what my brother said, but I can't stop myself from replaying his words in my head. It's hard to believe how much has changed over the last few months since Stella and I exchanged vows on this dock. I have to admit that with each day that passes, it feels more and more impossible to walk away from her at the end of the year.

I spend a moment trying to picture letting her go when the time comes, but instead, all I can think about is the happy little shimmy she does when she takes the first sip of her energy drink in the morning. I think about how beautiful she looks when she comes around my cock, and how she smiles each time Duke runs into our room at the end of the day and maneuvers his way between us to cuddle in bed. I think about how excited she gets each time the Hideaway gets a new booking or the hotel hits a new follower count on social media, and I know I'm completely gone for her.

Throughout all of this, no matter how hard I try, I can't imagine signing divorce papers in ten months. No part of me can picture going back to my small apartment and telling myself that what Stella and I have doesn't mean anything at the end of the year.

The longer I think about it, the more I realize I'm completely in love with Stella Hale.

Fuck. This isn't how this was supposed to go, but as soon as the thought crosses my mind, I know it's true. I've been falling for Stella since the first day she walked back into my life, and now I'm too invested to even imagine pulling away.

After spending most of my life not letting the people around me get too close, I should be terrified by how far I've allowed this to go. But I know that even if this all goes to shit, I'll never regret falling for Stella. She brings out the best parts of me. All summer I've admired the way she took over the hotel that was sad and empty and filled it with love and excitement. The more I think about it, the more I realize she did the same thing for me. Truthfully, the only thing that scares me more than the thought of losing her is going back to the person I was before she came into my life.

Blinking, I realize I've spent the last ten minutes wiping down the same seat, lost in my thoughts. Shaking my head, I try to clear my thoughts, but it's useless. Now that I've come to terms with how I really feel about Stella, all I can think about is convincing her to stay with me after this year is over.

A part of me knows that I shouldn't rush into anything—I mean, after all, I have months to convince her before we have to make a decision. But I know there's no way I can spend the rest of this year not knowing how she feels about me.

I take a breath and try to force myself to slow down, but it's no use. I know this could go terribly wrong, but suddenly I can't convince myself to wait. Throwing the barely used rag back in the glove box, I step off of the boat and head to my truck.

I guess now's as good of a time as any to tell my wife I'm in love with her.

CHAPTER 23
STELLA

"Thank you so much for coming. We hope you enjoyed your stay," I tell the couple checking out, as I hand them their final bill.

"Oh, yes. Everything was wonderful. We've already booked our stay for next year," the wife gushes, and I feel a swell of pride rise inside of me at how well the hotel's doing.

"I'm so happy to hear that. We look forward to seeing you again soon. Be safe traveling," I say, sitting down behind the counter as they make their way outside.

Today has been one of the longest days I've had since I started at the hotel. A bingo tournament pulled most of our volunteers away for the day, which left Avery and me to run everything. Thankfully I was able to get one of the housekeepers we recently hired to come in and turn over the rooms, but Avery and I have filled all the other responsibilities on our own. On top of that, I didn't manage to get much sleep last night—my mind was too consumed with the revelation that I'm actually in love with my husband—and my body is feeling it today.

I reach down and check the time on my phone, sighing in relief when I see it's almost seven. Chloe agreed to take the evening shift for me tonight, and she just sent me a text that she's on her way. All I can think about is how much I'm looking forward to eating dinner and taking a shower when Wyatt pushes into the lobby.

"Oh, hey," I say, smiling at him as he makes his way over.

"Hey, Stels. Are you almost done here?"

"Yeah, I'll be good to go as soon as Chloe gets here. Everything okay?"

"Oh, everything's fine. I just wanted to talk to you about something. But it's no big deal. I'll wait for you at the cottage," he says, and I notice he's fidgeting with his wedding band.

"Are you sure everything's okay? You seem nervous about something."

His eyes widen and he shakes his head. "Nope, I'm good. I'll see you at home in a few."

"Okay," I say, still trying to figure out what's gotten into him. "I'll see you then."

He leaves, and I spend the next few minutes wracking my brain for what he could want to talk to me about. I thought that everything was going so well between us, and he seemed happy spending time with me, but a wave of anxiety rolls through me at the thought of him deciding to end things between us.

Before I can start to spiral, Chloe walks in through the front door of the lobby, and I sigh in relief.

"Hey, Stella. How are you tonight?" she asks, sliding onto the stool beside me.

"I'm good. Honestly, just exhausted. It's been a crazy day here."

"No worries, you head on out and I'll meet you for brunch

tomorrow morning. We can chat then," she offers, and I smile at her appreciatively.

"Sounds good. Thank you again for doing this. You seriously saved me today."

"No problem. I didn't work today so I spent the day napping. I promise I'm good to go. I'll take care of everything."

"Thank you again. Miss Clara will be back tomorrow, and she should be in pretty early. And I'll get you a check next week for all the hours you've been putting in."

"Perfect, now you go get some rest, babe," she says, shooing me out from behind the counter.

I grab my bag and head toward the cottage, trying to convince myself I'm getting worked up over nothing. But by the time I reach the front door, I feel like my heart is going to beat out of my chest.

I push the door open, and pause when I hear Wyatt talking from the bedroom. "…totally in love with you and I can't imagine spending a single day without you," he says. I feel like my heart stops at the words.

What the hell?

I burst into the bedroom, not sure exactly what I'm expecting to find, but it definitely isn't Wyatt sitting on the bed talking to my chocolate lab. He looks up at me in surprise and I freeze, trying to piece together what's going on.

"Wait, what? When did you get here? I didn't hear you come in," he asks.

"Were you just telling Duke that you're in love with him," I blurt, unable to stop myself.

Wyatt blinks and I wait for him to say something before he groans. "Oh my god, tell me you didn't hear that."

"I definitely did, and I'd love to know what the hell is going on."

"Damn it," Wyatt mutters before confessing, "I was in here talking to your dog like a fool, practicing how to tell you that I'm completely in love with you when you walked in and heard me."

I freeze, unsure if I heard him right. "You...you love me?"

He stands and makes his way over to me, pulling me into his arms as he sits back on the bed. "Fuck, I feel like an idiot. I realized tonight I'm completely in love with you, Stella. And I know it's not what we agreed upon and I probably should wait until we've spent more of the year together, but I just need you to know that I love you and I don't ever want to let you go."

I remain silent, trying to let his words sink in as he continues to ramble. "I can't ask you to stay married to me if it's not what you want. But I'm just asking if we can give this a real shot, because you've become the most important person in my life and I can't imagine letting you walk away at the end of this year."

"Wait, you're in love with me?" I ask, trying to keep up with how fast he's talking.

"Yes, Stella, I'm completely in love with you. This was absolutely not how I saw this going, but I guess nothing about us has been conventional so why start now, right?"

I stare at him for a moment before his words finally register and I feel my face break into a smile. Running toward him, I wrap him in a hug and lean up to press a kiss to his mouth. "Wyatt, I'm in love with you too. I spent all night last night trying to figure out how to tell you because I can't stand the thought of this thing ending between us in ten months either.

"Oh, thank god." He sighs before bringing his mouth to mine and kisses me hard. Before I can get too lost in the moment, Duke barks behind us and moves to nudge me in the leg with his nose.

"Are you feeling left out, sweet boy?" I ask with a laugh. "You know we love you too."

Our dog barks again and both Wyatt and I lean down to pet him. After a moment, Wyatt asks me, "Should we try this whole thing again? I wanted it to be a little more romantic, but I got nervous and went and screwed it all up."

"Nope, it was perfect," I say, leaning in to let him hold me in his arms. "Never a dull moment, right?"

"COME ON, Duke, we need to clean this place," I tell my pup, looking around at the cottage I've neglected to clean for the last week. Wyatt and I slept late after spending most of the night kissing and fucking, and he left a few minutes ago to grab our groceries for the week before we meet our friends for brunch.

I'm giving myself a mental pep talk to get off the couch and start on the mountain of laundry that's accumulated when my phone pings.

> Avery: We got three more bookings overnight. The second week of March for next year is officially booked already for spring break.

> Stella: Shut up!

> Stella: Are you serious?

Avery: Yep, I checked twice to make sure. I
think we're gonna need to up our search for
more staff.

Avery: The knitting club ladies are great, but
Miss Clara almost took out one of the guests
with her cane on accident yesterday and
Miss Eleanor keeps hitting on the guests.

Stella: Shit, okay. I'll ask around and see if
we can get the listings pushed out to some
of the neighboring towns. And up the ads
we're doing online too.

Avery: Already taken care of.

Stella: You're the best.

Avery: I know ;) See you in an hour.

After reading her text, I throw my phone onto the sofa, start the washing machine, and run the vacuum through the living room.

"Duke, I love you, but between the sand you track in and all the shedding, I don't think I'm ever keeping this house clean," I say, pausing to empty out the vacuum for the second time.

My dog lets out a loud sigh at my feet and rolls onto his back, looking over at me expectantly. I bend down and pat his stomach with a laugh. "I know, I know. I'm not complaining. But it's a good thing you're cute," I tease.

After running the vacuum for a while longer and finally deciding the floors will have to do for now, I turn to the book-cases in the living room that are still full of Memaw's romance novels. I've avoided them for the last two months, feeling like going near them is the last remaining hurdle for coming to terms with her really being gone. But even from the other side of the room, I can tell the shelves are covered in a light coat of dust, and today feels like as good of a day as any to knock this off the to-do list.

I spend a few minutes going through the stacks as I dust the shelves, and I smile at some of the fun names on the titles in front of me. I take one off the shelf and flip through it, immediately noticing my grandmother's loopy cursive in the margins throughout all the pages. It makes me smile when I read her thoughts, and for the first time since she passed, I feel like I have a little piece of her back.

"God, Memaw, you really were one of a kind, weren't you? I guess I've got some reading to do, huh?" I whisper as my eyes catch on a cream envelope peeking out of an alien romance.

Pulling it out, I feel my breath catch as I see my name written in all caps across the front. Taking a steady breath, I tear open the envelope and start to read.

Stella,

Hi, my sweet girl. I hope this letter finds you happily married and running this hotel with all the determination and excitement you've met every other challenge and opportunity with. But I couldn't go without leaving you this note, further explaining the choices I've made.

By the time you read this, I'm certain you'll have made a decision on what to do with the Hideaway. You know an old hag like me couldn't go without having a little fun with this old place. But I want you to know whatever you decide to do, I'm so proud of you.

I worried for months that you may hate me for the decisions my final wishes required you to make, but I knew if you had the option to keep the Hideaway without ever stepping foot back here, you would take it. I hope you can forgive me but just know all I've ever wanted is what's best for you.

I also knew if I let you take this on by yourself, you'd lose yourself in running this place and forget to fall in love or see your friends along the way. I hoped the provision of marriage forced you to find someone to shoulder some of this weight with. And I've always said there's just a little bit of magic in the walls of this hotel, so I selfishly hoped these walls would lead you to your soulmate the same way it led me to your pops all those years ago. But if not, I hope you at least found a friend to make you smile and keep you from withdrawing away from the rest of the world when times get tough.

Over the last few years, I've watched you lose a lot of the light you had for life. You took on everyone else's problems and let the world dim a lot of that sunshine you always had inside you.

But, my sweet girl, if you can promise this old woman anything, promise me you won't ever stop searching for sunshine. Storms can come along and shake us to our core, but they don't have to define us.

*I hope that moving here reminded you that some-
times you have to choose yourself, and in doing so,
it's also okay to ask for help from your friends.*

*I love you so much, my girl. Keep choosing joy
and keep choosing you.*

All my love always,

Memaw

*P.S.—Just in case my intuition was right on who
you picked to marry, tell Wyatt I said thank you for
taking care of my girl. You two always had something special, and I hate that Meredith and I aren't
there to give you shit for how right we always were
about the two of you.*

I finish the letter, wiping tears from my eyes. Duke comes over and licks my leg in concern, and I pat his head. "It's okay, buddy. These are happy tears."

I reread the letter again and I can't help but smile at how well my grandmother knew me. She had no way of knowing I'd lose my teaching job at the same time I had to make a decision about the Hideaway, but I know she's right. If she hadn't put any of the stipulations in place, I probably would have taken ownership of the hotel and continued to avoid this place. And I definitely would have tried to do it by myself.

Just as I'm wiping the last of my stray tears, the front door opens and Wyatt walks inside.

"Hey, Stels, I missed you today. I thought we could—" he starts, dropping his keys on the table by the door and stopping when he sees my tear-stained face. "What the hell happened? Are you okay?"

He rushes over to me and I smile at him. "I promise, I'm fine. I was cleaning and I just found this letter that Memaw hid for me."

I hold it out to him and he takes it, reading it quickly and smiling when he finishes. "Damn, that woman really was something. But she's right. My granny was always swearing up and down that we'd end up together. She actually pressured me to reach out to you right before she died, but I was already dealing with so much here, it just didn't seem like the right time."

"Well, thanks to Memaw's scheming, it worked out anyway," I tell him, dropping a quick kiss on his lips. "Now, are you ready to break the news to our friends that this fake marriage actually isn't so fake anymore?"

Wyatt groans and runs his hand over his face. "God, don't get me wrong, Stels, I'm so happy we've worked this out between us, but what if we just don't tell them anything? They're never gonna let me hear the end of this."

I giggle at his expression and pretend to think about it. "Well, we definitely don't have to tell them. But there's no way I'm keeping this from Avery. Do you think she can keep it a secret?"

"Fuck, we definitely have to tell them."

"That's what I thought," I say with a laugh. "Now, let's get ready to go."

CHAPTER 24
WYATT

"Hale, party of seven," the hostess yells. Stella waves her hand.

"That's us," she calls, and we follow her to a large corner booth that looks out over the ocean.

"This place is so cute," Chloe says, and Avery and Stella nod in agreement.

"I bet some of our bachelorette groups will love this place for Saturday brunch," Stella agrees.

Avery pulls out her phone and taps away in her notes. "Yeah, that's a good idea. I'm adding a reminder to include this place as a suggested restaurant on the handout we give everyone at check-in."

"Damn, the two of you really think of everything," Trent says, and Avery shrugs.

"We try. So far, we've had some happy customers and they've already started booking for next summer, so it seems to be paying off."

"That's awesome. We've already seen a huge increase in sales at the store," Bennett says.

"Same thing with The Sand Bar," Everett agrees.

"So, speaking of next year, have the two of you decided what you're gonna do with the hotel once this whole fake marriage thing is over?" Trent asks, and everyone goes quiet as they wait for our response.

"Uh, funny you should ask," Stella starts, looking at me and I nod for her to continue. "We actually finally decided there's nothing fake about what's between us."

The table goes silent before Avery lets out an excited screech. "I fucking knew it."

"About damn time," Bennett mutters and Chloe cheers in agreement.

Stella and I both laugh at the reaction before Trent asks, "Wait, so just to be clear—you two are finally admitting there's something real between you, right?"

I resist the urge to roll my eyes. "Yes, dumbass, that's what we just said."

"Hell yeah, I won the bet," he yells and Stella and I look at each other in confusion.

"Bet?" I ask, looking between my brothers and best friend. "What the fuck are you talking about?"

"There may have been a friendly wager between us," Bennett answers, refusing to look at me.

"On what, exactly?" I ask, waiting for them to fess up.

"We made a bet on how long it would take for you to pull your head out of your asses and admit that the two of you wanted to be together."

Stella laughs, and I mutter "Asshole" under my breath.

"What was everyone's guess?" Stella asks and everyone goes quiet.

"I said two weeks," Avery admits. "So y'all held out a hell of a lot longer than I thought."

"Chloe said a month," Bennett says. "And I said six months, so I was clearly super fucking off."

"I obviously guessed two months," Trent says. "Which means I won."

"What was your guess?" I ask Everett.

"No offense, Stella, but my bet was that he finally decided to take Miss Eleanor up on her offer."

I flip him off, and the rest of the table erupts into laughter at that.

"None taken," Stella says. "Honestly, I keep waiting on it too."

"Y'all are such a pain in my ass," I mutter, knowing I don't mean it.

The waitress brings our order of mimosas and bloody mary's. As soon as everyone has a drink, Stella grabs her glass.

"Here's to a lifetime full of booked hotels and busy businesses," she says, holding her glass up to the rest of us.

"I'll drink to that," Avery says, as the rest of us clink glasses.

🌴🌴🌴🌴🌴

"Can you believe our friends placed bets against us this whole time?" I ask Stella as we make our way inside the cottage after brunch.

"No, I'm actually not the least bit surprised," Stella says with a laugh.

"Yeah, I guess," I murmur. "But I still think it's rude."

Stella shakes her head. "Babe, I hate to break it to you, but have you met our friends? They love giving us shit, and the way you let them annoy you makes you a little bit of an easy target."

"Yeah, whatever. Anyway, enough about them," I tell her, reaching down to pick her up and winding her legs around my hips. "Can I please fuck my wife?"

Stella smiles at me, and pretends to think about it. "Hmm, I guess I'll allow it," she teases, reaching between us to palm my dick through my shorts.

As soon as I step into the bedroom, I toss her on the bed and start tugging my shirt over my head. Stella smiles up at me from her position on the bed, and I reach down to run my hand through her hair before leaning down to press a quick kiss against her lips.

After I kiss her, I push her down against the bed, pushing her skirt up until I can see her pink panties.

I graze my finger down the front of them and smile when I feel how she's dripping for me.

"Is my wife desperate to be fucked?" I ask as I pull them down. Stella murmurs in agreement.

After teasing her for a moment, I reach into the bedside drawer and grab her vibrator, clicking it on and pressing it against her clit in one quick move. She squeaks out a sound of surprise as I continue to tease her with it.

I spend the next few minutes getting her close to the edge before pulling back until she's a mess and begging for me to fuck her.

"All you had to do was ask," I tease, keeping her vibrator pressed against her clit while I push my pants down and slide inside her. I can tell that neither of us are going to last like this, so I push in and out of her fast, groaning as I feel her pussy tighten around my cock.

"Yes, Wyatt, I'm close," she mutters, and I press the button to make the toy go to the next setting. Stella squeals at the new sensations, and I feel her spasm against me with her orgasm. I follow her over the edge, spilling inside her.

"Shit," she mutters. "I don't think I'll ever get tired of this," she says with a smile as I pull out of her, smiling as I watch my cum leak out of her.

"Damn, that's hot," I mutter before looking back at her. "And I guess it's a good thing we've got forever to find out, huh?"

EPILOGUE

STELLA

TEN MONTHS LATER

appy anniversary, Stels," Wyatt says, pushing into the bedroom, carrying a tray with two plates, both piled with pancakes and bacon.

"Good morning, hubby. And happy anniversary to you too," I say, wiping the sleep from my eyes and taking the energy drink he's holding out for me.

"I can't believe it's been a year since we got married. Did you ever think we'd end up here when you agreed to all of this?" he asks, sitting the tray down on the bed between us.

"I definitely didn't see all of this coming, but I'm so glad we ended up where we did. I— Oh my goodness, Duke, you've gotta stop," I say, turning my attention to our lab who keeps pawing the bed, obviously excited by the smell of the food. He ignores me and jumps on the bed, tail wagging, and tries to sneak a piece of bacon off our plates.

Wyatt just rolls his eyes at the pup and throws him a piece before turning his attention back to me. "So do you want your present now or later?"

"Is that even a question? Gimme," I tease before adding, "but I kinda feel like an asshole, because I thought we agreed on no gifts."

"We did. But this isn't really an anniversary gift. It's just something I want you to have," he tells me, standing and searching through his bedside table before pulling out a small ring box.

I look at him in surprise as he bends down to one knee beside the bed and opens the box, revealing a gorgeous vintage ring. I stare at it for a moment before I realize it looks familiar.

"Is that my Memaw's?" I choke out, tears already clogging my throat.

"Yeah, apparently she had one more trick up her sleeve." He laughs, and I wait for him to explain.

"I got a call from Mr. Marshall about two weeks ago asking me to come by the office. Apparently, your grandmother left instructions for him to contact your husband at the end of the year and give it to him. Or if you'd decided not to stay married, he said he was supposed to call you. Either way, none of that really matters. And I know we're already married but you deserve a real proposal and a real ring. So, Stella Hale Robinson, will you be my real wife?"

I laugh, wiping a tear from my eye before nodding. "Of course, I will."

"Thank god," he mutters, slipping the ring on my finger. "And I also thought we could take a real honeymoon this time…what do you think?"

"Really?" I ask, my eyes wide. "I would love that. But where should we go?"

"Wherever you want," Wyatt answers. "Now that we've hired on a full staff, I feel like we can take a little time off. Where do you want to go? Barbados? Aruba? The Maldives?"

I squeal in excitement, before saying, "Oh my gosh, this is going to be so fun! But wait, who will watch Duke and Stan?"

I look over to see Stan, our lizard friend, sunning in the window sill and laugh a little at the question. We'd never intended to make him a pet, but after the sixth visit from the exterminator, we finally gave in and admitted defeat.

"I think Stan will be fine on his own. He's a big boy and he's used to taking care of himself," Wyatt points out, and I giggle.

"Yeah, you're probably right. And I'm sure Avery will be happy to keep Duke. I know she loves when she gets to spend time with him," I admit, cutting off a piece of my pancake and popping it into my mouth.

"Perfect. As soon as you pick, we'll start planning and we can go in the fall as soon as our busy season ends."

"This is going to be the best time," I gush. "But are you sure you don't want to pick?"

"Nope, as long as I'm with you, I don't care," Wyatt says, reaching over and kissing me.

"Aww, who knew you were such a romantic. I personally never saw that grumpy side of you that everyone loved to tease you about, but what would the town say if they knew about this side of you?" I tell him, and he rolls his eyes.

"They don't need to know, because I've already found the only one I want to be with."

I smile. "We better not let Miss Eleanor find out or she might key my car."

"Eh, yeah, that's possible," he teases, and I push the food to the side so I can kiss him.

We've only been kissing a few seconds when I hear a knock on the front door. "I swear to god, if that's Avery… That woman has a radar for when I'm about to get some," my husband mutters, and I laugh as I throw back the comforter and grab my robe to cover my pajamas.

"I don't know who it is. If it's her, she didn't text me that she was coming over," I say, swinging the door open and pausing when I see a woman in an elegant white wedding dress standing at the front door.

At first I worry that I forgot about one of our weddings this weekend, but as soon as I look at the girl's face, I know that's not what's going on. She's got tears and mascara streaked down both cheeks, and I don't miss the slightly panicked way she's looking around right now. It takes a moment for my brain to recognize her, but eventually I realize it's Hailey, the girl from the first bachelorette trip.

"Oh my gosh, Hailey. Are you okay?" I ask, opening the door wider for her.

"Stella, I'm so sorry," she cries. "But yesterday was supposed to be my wedding and I just couldn't do it. I couldn't marry him. So, I got in the car and I ran. I had no idea where to go and I told myself I wasn't going to take you up on your offer to move here, but I got scared and just started driving. I can leave if you want me to. I know this is absolutely crazy. I just really didn't know what else to do."

"You're okay," I tell Hailey, wrapping my arm around her. "Just take a deep breath. You know, not too long ago, this was the place I came to when I was feeling a little lost. And I think it could be the same for you. Why don't you come inside, and we'll figure something out?"

WANT MORE FROM CRESTBROOK COVE?

Hailey's story is coming early 2026. Preorder the ebook here.

ACKNOWLEDGMENTS

Wow, I can't believe we're already here again. The writing process for each book is always so different, but one thing that never changes is the fact that I have the most incredible friends and family. Without them, none of this would be possible, and I'm so grateful for all the support.

First of all, to my sweet husband—I think I fall a little more in love with you with every book I write. You've been my anchor through every storm, and you've seen me through some of the darkest times over the last year. Thanks for always searching for the sunshine with me, even when it's hard. I love you forever, C.

To my sweet Mom and Dad, thank you for always pushing me to be my best and giving me encouragement when I need a break. I'm so grateful for every packing party and every post office run. You've always encouraged me to go after the things I want, and none of this would be possible without your support. And Nonnie and Dah, thank you for always cheering the loudest for books you've never read. Your support means the absolute world to me. I'm endlessly grateful for the four of you and I love you always.

My girl, Cassie— how did I ever do this without you? You are the most encouraging and helpful friend I could ask for, and I adore getting to work with you. Thank you for the endless graphics and voice memo support.

Rae, thank you so much for helping me manage so much

behind the scenes. I'm so grateful for your advice and the fact that you usually know what I need before I even think to ask for it.

Emma, you sweet angel. Thank you so much for putting up with every tag and voice memo throughout this whole process. I'm not exaggerating when I say this book wouldn't exist with out your support. Every time I considered deleting everything, you came through and saved the day, and I will never be able to thank you enough.

Erica, thank you so much for dealing with my chaos and cleaning up my messy words. I adore working with you, and I'm so grateful for your friendship.

Brittni, as always, you just get me and my characters, and I'm so grateful every time we get to work together. Thank you so much for your encouragement and your assistance in making this story the best it can be.

To my sweet betas—Hunter, Emily, and Lillian—y'all make writing so fun! I look forward to reading all your unhinged comments, and you always know exactly what I'm missing.

Caroline, thank you for being patient with me when everything in my world went off the rails and making sure this book was still perfect. You're truly the best.

To all the author friends that encouraged me when I got scared of trying something new, I couldn't do this without you. I can't thank you enough for your support. And a special thank you to Ambar for helping me make this story the best it could be and always being there when I needed to vent. ILYSM.

To my ARC readers and the best street team in the world, y'all are such a fabulous hype team, and I can't thank you enough for your enthusiasm for these characters. Every tag, review, and post means the absolute world to me, and I'll never be able to thank you enough.

And finally, to you my sweet reader, truly none of this is possible without you. Thank you so much for taking a chance on my stories, and I hope you never stop searching for your own sunshine. Thank you for joining me in Crestbrook Cove.

LIST OF CONTENT WARNINGS

Off page death of a loved one
Mentions of anxiety and panic attacks
Explicit sexual content
Explicit language

ABOUT THE AUTHOR

Hollie Luckie is a small town girl that wholeheartedly believes in happily ever afters. Between teaching English and writing romance, she is always getting lost in a fictional world. She resides in south Alabama with her high school sweetheart, her dog Memphis, and her own farm of quirky farm animals. You can find Hollie on Instagram at @authorhollieluckie or on Goodreads.

ALSO BY HOLLIE LUCKIE

Springside Series

Where We Break

Why We Break

What We Build - Coming late 2025

Deer Valley Inn Series

Matchmaking Under The Mistletoe

Crestbrook Cove Series

Searching for Sunshine

WTS- Coming Spring 2026

BE THE FIRST TO KNOW

Want to stay up to date on all the things? Join my newsletter, sign up for alerts on upcoming signings, and follow my reader group here!